Reunited

Anna's Story

By

Ronna M. Bacon

Deuteronomy 31:6 Be strong and of a good courage, fear not, nor be afraid of them: for the LORD your God, he it is that does go with you; he will not fail you, nor forsake you.

Psalm 9:9-10 The LORD also will be a refuge for the oppressed, a refuge in times of trouble. And they that know your name will put their trust in you: for you, LORD, have not forsaken them that seek you.

Table of Contents

The mid-summer daytime air hung heavy and moisture laden. It was one of those summer days when it felt as if the air was ready to mourn and cry, the sun hidden to some extent behind the haziness of the sky. Anna Koyle stood for a moment on her back porch, an arm wrapped around one of the white-painted columns. She had just returned home from a wedding in their church and had spent time with her brother, his wife, and her three triplet nephews and their families. A soft smile creased her face as she thought of the little ones: Arlyn's young daughter, Briar's young son, and the surprise that Cayce and his wife had kept hidden, their twins, a son and a daughter.

Anna walked down the four wooden steps to the patio, her bare feet relishing the coolness of the stone and then the grass as she stepped onto the fresh-cut lawn. She paused, feeling something off or odd about the day before she shrugged. After having the triplets go through what they termed as their adventures, life and death as they were, she was uneasy. Something big was about to happen and Anna was afraid suddenly. No, she decided, not just afraid. It went much deeper than that.

Walking through the backyard and then heading for the front yard, Anna hesitated for a moment. Something was telling her that once she stepped past the front edge of the house, her life would change. She felt the danger waiting for her out there. Anna hesitated for a moment with her face upturned to the sky. Her heart raised in prayer as she petitioned her Heavenly Father to protect her. Anna had no reason to pray this way but she did.

Anna's gaze was focused on the grass. She loved the feel of fresh-mown grass under her bare feet. She always had. Even in her forties, Anna refused to wear shoes if she could get away without them. She paused for a moment, a frown crossing her face before her eyes raised.

Staring at the man standing in front of her, Anna didn't take in the bouquet of peach roses held in the man's hands. She looked up, knowing that the man was tall. A hand covered her mouth to still her scream. It couldn't be, could it? This was not Jeremiah Riley standing in front of her after over twenty years!

"Jeremiah? Jeremiah Riley? Is that really you?" Anna took a step backwards, shaken to the core of her being. This man had disappeared so many years ago and she had not had a single word from him. Shock covered her face as she stared at Jeremiah. "Where have you been?"

Jeremiah Riley stood and stared at the lady in front of him. She was even more beautiful than he remembered. She had faint lines now etched on her face and a few silver threads in the deep auburn curls that he had dreamed about for so many years. Her deep hazel eyes held the questions that she would not ask.

"Anna? Is this really you? I'm sorry. I didn't mean to be gone for so long." Jeremiah ran his hand through the close-dropped blond curls and then rubbed at the reddish beard that was neatly trimmed. His deep blue eyes assessed her before he looked around. Jeremiah could sense the danger approaching them, danger that had kept him a prisoner for so many years, preventing him from returning to his home and yes, to the woman who he had pledged his love to all those many years ago.

Anna stared up at him again, her hand reaching for the ring that hung on a gold chain around her neck. She had never gotten rid of it, praying that at some point she would have peace that she could. That peace had never happened.

"Jeremiah? Where were you? I looked so hard for you for months but had no idea what had happened to you." Anna didn't move towards him. She didn't know the man any more, the man who had claimed her heart all those years ago. "What happened?"

"What happened? It's a long story, Anna, and I don't know that we have the time to tell it." Jeremiah reached for her hand, tugging her towards the road. He stared down at her feet. "You don't have shoes on!"

"No, I don't. I wasn't planning on going anywhere." Anna stared at him and then down at her feet before she was running around the house and finding her sandals. She paused to grab her phone, tucking it into a pocket and grabbing her keys. She locked the door behind her before she was running back towards Jeremiah.

Jeremiah had spent those few moments turning in a circle, trying to determine just where the threat was coming from that he could feel. He was free from his captors at long last, having spent over twenty years

—

kept locked away in a compound outside of the country. Someone had appeared four months before and whisked him away to freedom and then back to his home. Jeremiah knew that his family would want to see him, those who were still alive. But the first person he wanted to see? That was Anna, the lady who had claimed his heart all those years ago and who had promised to be his sweetheart for life.

Turning as he felt Anna nearby, he reached for her hand and tugged her with him. Seating her into his vehicle, Jeremiah watched her through the window before he was around the car and behind the wheel, driving away to find somewhere they could talk. And talk they would. He had a story to tell her, one that he didn't know if she would even believe.

"Jeremiah?" Anna's voice was quiet and halting. She didn't know how to ask what she wanted to know, other than to just verbalize it. "Was there another woman?"

Jeremiah shot her a quick glance before his head was shaking violently.

"Never, Anna. I would not do that to you. I was kidnapped and then held captive overseas for all these years. Four months ago, someone appeared, freed me, and then helped me to get home." Jeremiah's voice was sober. "I wouldn't do that, Anna. You are the only one for me." He pulled into a parking lot, staring at the trails that led away from it. "We spent a lot of time here. I would come back here in my dreams but you were never here with me. I spent so much time dreaming of trying to find you and never doing that."

"You did? I prayed for you for so many years. I didn't want to stop doing that even if you had walked away from me." Anna's face was sober. She was uncertain as to what to expect from Jeremiah. "Where were you?"

Jeremiah sighed and then began to pray. He had to tell Anna his story and then hear hers. He just didn't know if they would have time for that before he disappeared again and Anna disappeared too.

"We'll talk, Anna. We need to pray, though. The ones who held me? They won't willingly let me return here and to you." He held out a hand, waiting patiently for Anna to decide if she would take it or not.

Anna studied Jeremiah's face and then his outstretched hand. She didn't know what to do. Her eyes lifted to the sky that she could see outside of the window, in conversation with her Abba Father. She nodded at last, her hand reaching for Jeremiah's.

"I trust you, Jeremiah. I know the character of who you were. I just need to learn the character of who you are now." Anna looked past Jeremiah, screaming as their doors were wrenched open and they were pulled roughly from the vehicle and then shoved along one of the paths in front of them. They disappeared into the foliage, no sign of their having passed that way remaining.

Chapter 2

The next morning, Anna's brother, Ardan, shifted on his chair, turning to try and find his sister. Bessie's hand rested on his arm, a frown on her face. She too was looking for her sister-in-law. The triplets and their families were around their parents, all of them watching for Anna.

"Where's Anna?" Bessie kept her voice low in the rustling that was going on pre-service.

"I don't know. She planned to be here." Ardan shifted to face Bessie, seeing the concern on her face and on the boys' faces. Their ladies had their attention on the little ones.

"I know that she did." Bessie pulled out her phone from her purse and scrolled through her messages. "I didn't receive any message from her since Friday. That is odd. She'll let us know if she's not coming."

Ardan nodded, his attention taken by the movement at the front of the sanctuary.

"We'll stop by there after the service. Maybe she's sick and had muted her phone." All Ardan could do at that point was pray for his sister before his attention was taken by the message. They had a new minister, the previous minister having been the one who had threatened Cayce and Haley. His messages were straight from the Bible and were causing the members of his church to search out his words and agree or disagree with him. The growth was becoming obvious to those outside of the church and the church was growing as more people sought to find the answers to life that God offered them.

Ardan approached Anna's house just after noon on the Sunday. Joe, a police detective and close friend, was at his side. Ardan unlocked the front door and disengaged the security system. Joe's hand on his arm stopped his forward steps.

"Let me go through first, Ardan. And then I'll walk you through the house." Joe stared him down until Ardan nodded. Joe walked through the house, not finding anything out of the ordinary. "Ardan? Would Anna have taken a purse?" He appeared back in front of Ardan as he asked his question.

"No, she used her phone case for most things." Ardan walked through the house as well. "She kept her debit card and credit card in her purse but used a pay app on her phone if she didn't want to carry either one. Her license would be in her phone case and the insurance and car ownership in the glove box of her car." Ardan spun in a circle before he walked back to the kitchen. His fingers touched the charging cable for Anna's phone. "She never leaves her charger like this." He reached to unplug it before Joe could stop him.

"Okay, Ardan. Back outside and with Bessie. I need to bring in a team." Joe walked away to stand on the front porch, his phone to his ear as he called in a team to search. The family didn't need this, he knew, not after what Arlyn, Briar, and Cayce had gone through.

—

Bessie was out of the car and in her husband's arms as he stopped in front of her. He turned slightly to study Anna's home and then the vehicles on the street. Ardan sighed. He had no idea if any of the vehicles didn't belong there.

"Ardan? Is she in there?" Bessie was afraid that Anna was in there and was dead.

"No, she's not. Her phone is gone but I don't know where she is. Her dress from earlier yesterday is thrown on her bed. That's unusual for her." Ardan turned Bessie back to the car and made her sit. He stood with an arm on the open door and the other one on the top of the car.

"It is." Bessie wrung her hands in desperation. "We don't need Anna to disappear. We had enough of that already in our family." Her phone was in her hand as she read the text message from Arlyn. "Arlyn's looking for us."

Ardan sighed before he reached for his wife's phone and sent off a text message to the triplets. He handed the phone back to Bessie, his eyes on the house. He questioned where his sister was and could only pray that she was alive and safe. Somehow, he didn't think that she was safe.

"Ardan? Has Anna ever said anything about Jeremiah over the years? They were so close back in their twenties. I expected them to marry but then Jeremiah just dropped out of sight."

Ardan stared down at his wife, his thoughts tumbling over themselves. Anna and Jeremiah had been close at one time, he knew, and everyone had expected them to marry. But then, Jeremiah disappeared without a trace no matter how much they looked for him. Anna had said nothing about their relationship, which didn't surprise Ardan. She was like that.

"We all did. We just never could figure out what happened. We searched for him as best as we could at the time. And Anna never said anything. She grieved and then seemed to just move on with her life." Ardan had tried to find out how Anna was feeling but his sister would just hug him and walk away.

Joe hesitated to approach the older couple. He was good friends with their sons and their wives and had grown up moving in and out of the Koyle home. This time it was different. This time, he was investigating yet another disappearance involving his friends.

"Joe?" Bessie was out of the car and standing in front of him. "What can you tell us?"

Joe looked at her, studied Ardan, and then raised his eyes to see Arlyn, Briar, and Cayce waiting at the police tape, their wives and children with them. He sighed. He didn't know what to tell them other than that Anna was missing and there was no clue as to where she was. Her security feed would be looked at but he didn't know if it would show anything at all.

"She's not there, Ardan. I don't see that there is anything that would say where she was." Joe hesitated before continuing. "We need to look at her security feed."

—

Ardan nodded, already assuming that would be the case.

"I have it loaded on my phone. Anna asked for that." Ardan handed over his phone, the security feed ready for Joe.

Joe searched through it, pausing as he saw a man approaching Anna. He frowned. He tilted the phone towards Ardan.

"Do you know who this is?" Joe thought the man looked familiar but he wasn't sure.

Ardan stared at the still photo, a frown on his face. He could feel Bessie leaning against him.

"That's Jeremiah!" Bessie's voice held the shock that they both felt. "Where has he been?"

"Jeremiah?" Joe's head spun to stare at Bessie. "As in Jeremiah Riley?"

Bessie nodded, frowning even harder. Where had he been? They needed to find him. If they found him, maybe they would find Anna. Jeremiah had simply disappeared over twenty years ago, with no word. He and Anna had been a couple, a couple that everyone expected to marry. Anna had not said much after he disappeared, keeping her emotions and thoughts to herself. That was who Anna was.

Chapter 3

Bessie paced their home later that afternoon. Anna had not been found. Joe had been around not that long earlier, just to update them on what they had found. He had been disappointed and distraught that they had no news on what happened other than Anna had walked willingly away with Jeremiah. His question had been how close the two had been and another question had been if they had been in contact at all. No one had been able to confirm that. Only Anna could and she was missing.

"Ardan? What are your thoughts?" Bessie turned to find her husband just standing at the kitchen counter, staring out of the window above the sink.

"What do I think?" Ardan turned to find his wife standing behind him. He simply wrapped her into a hug. "I don't know what to think. Anna seemed to go willingly with Jeremiah. I want to know where he's been and why."

"She did, love. And I don't know why and I want to understand that." Bessie moved away from Ardan, seeing their sons and their families coming in the front door. "Boys? You're here?"

"We are, Mom." Arlyn spoke for the three of them. "We need to understand this. What didn't you tell us?"

"What didn't we tell you?" Ardan sighed even as he reached for his grandson. "I don't know what we aren't telling you. Anna never spoke of Jeremiah after he disappeared. We don't know how close they were although they had only ever dated each other."

"You were expecting them to marry?" Haley spoke up, sharing a look with Cayce.

"I think that we were. It seemed as if they had reached an agreement but we were never told that. Jeremiah just disappeared." Ardan shared a look with Bessie. Neither one had pried with Anna as to any decision she and Jeremiah might have made.

"I don't remember him at all." Briar reached past his mother for the coffee pot, pouring coffee for those who wanted it and then pouring tea for those who preferred that.

"You were too young, I think, Briar." Bessie hugged her son, not sure how to respond. "I think you were around five or six when he disappeared."

"I can remember him." Cayce spoke up. "He was always interested in what we were doing. I often wondered what happened to him."

Ardan nodded, moving to answer the door. He stared at the couple standing there for a moment before he stepped back to let them in.

"Abe? Emma? What are you two doing here?" He reached for Isaac as he jumped for him. "Where's your daughter?"

"With Eddie and Peg." Abe responded quickly, stating the names of his aunt and uncle. "What is going on? We were just heading this way for a quick visit, but something has happened."

"There has been. Anna disappeared yesterday afternoon. We had been together as a family just for a fun time. She was at home and then walked away with a man." Ardan rubbed at his face, finding Isaac hugging him.

"And do you know the man?" Emma reached for her phone, bringing up one of the programs that she used. She had a business that found people that no one else could find.

"We do. He's Jeremiah Riley. Anna and he were dating twenty some years ago. He disappeared on a work trip and just now reappeared. We don't know where he's been." Ardan nodded as Abe frowned at him. "He appears on Anna's security feed and then they walk away to his vehicle and he drives off. I had no idea that he was back in town."

"You didn't? That's a long time to disappear without a good reason." Emma frowned at Abe who simply smiled at her and shook his head. "Let me know what all you can about him."

"Later, Emma. For now, we're just meeting here as a family and then to spend some time in prayer." Ardan walked back towards the kitchen, Bessie reaching for Isaac. "Emma wants whatever information we can get to her about Jeremiah."

"And we will do that." Bessie reached to hug Emma and then Abe. "You two didn't come for that, did you?"

"No, we didn't. We actually came just to visit but you have a need for my work." Emma shook her head at Bessie. "You do. We'll get all the information

———

19

we need before we leave. For now, we will pray with you all.”

Late that afternoon, Cayce and Haley tucked their twins into their cribs and then stared at one another before Haley was moving to hug Cayce. Neither one felt that they had accomplished anything that afternoon, despite their work.

“Where is your aunt, Cayce?” Haley just held her husband, feeling the emotions roiling inside him.

“I wish I knew, sweetheart. I would go in and bring her home. All we can do is pray that she is alive and well.” Cayce blinked against the tears that were gathering in his eyes. “She’s always been there for us over the years. She never walked away from us. Not ever.”

“No, that’s not her character. She loves you too much to do that.” Haley turned slightly as one of the twins stirred and then settled down again. “We’re meeting tomorrow?”

“We are but not until the evening. We all have commitments that we can’t give up.” Cayce was frustrated at that. “I want to be out there searching for her.”

“We all do but we can’t. Joe is involved as the investigator. He’ll be back around many times with questions.”

Cayce turned them to walk from the twins’s room. “I just wish it was different. I want Aunt Anna home.”

Joe looked at the stack of papers that he had accrued over that day related to Anna. He had little information on Jeremiah other than that his parents were deceased. That made it much more difficult for him to investigate Jeremiah. He would need help from God, he decided, to decide where to start. And where to start meant finding that man and Anna.

Chapter 4

Anna had walked willingly away with Jeremiah that day, questions in her mind but still trusting that he meant her no harm. She studied him for a moment, not sure if she was doing the right thing. She had been in such a hurry that she forgot her phone, not missing it at all until later.

Jeremiah had tucked her into his truck and then driven to the park. He had walked her onto the pathway, knowing that men would be waiting for them. These men were his bodyguards for now. Jeremiah had begged for some time alone with Anna. He had waited, hardly daring to breathe before that request was granted with the stipulation that he bring her with him when he returned. They needed to keep her safe as well now that he was back in his hometown and approaching someone who had been very important to him in days past.

Anna had stared with horror as the three men had surrounded them and then walked them away from the park. She tried to dig in her heels and stop but Jeremiah's hand was firm on hers and pulled her with him. He simply shook his head at her as she opened her mouth to protest. Watching carefully as they were walked towards a home, Anna frowned. This house belonged to someone who had been absent from town for years. Everyone wondered who owned it. It was maintained, everyone knew but it still a mystery as to the owner. It was under a numbered company, everyone was aware of that.

Sitting quietly for the afternoon, Anna was finally on her feet, heading for the kitchen to try and find something for them to eat. Jeremiah had not spoken, other than to ask her to trust him. She had stared at him, shaking her head. How could she trust him now that he was back after so many years without any word from him? Her emotions were in a turmoil, as could only be expected. Anna paused as she saw one of the men turning from the stove, pointing to trays that he had prepared.

"Thank you." Anna turned from the room, carrying one of the trays, the man following her with the other. She hadn't expected this, not knowing how her nephews had been treated when they had been abducted.

Jeremiah turned from where he had been studying the back yard through the French doors that led to the yard from the office. He reached for the tray from the man to set it on the coffee table in from of the loveseat and then reached for the one that Anna was carrying. Jeremiah simply pointed to the loveseat, waiting for Anna to sit before he did. His hand went out without him thinking about it. Anna moved her hand away from him. She just didn't know him any more. She looked up for a moment, praying for safety and understanding but more importantly for protection. She had no idea what she was facing and that scared her.

Jeremiah sighed, knowing that Anna didn't trust him any more. It was a given as the young people would say. He just prayed for their meal and then for his friend. He didn't want to lose Anna again but that

---

was a real possibility. Jeremiah did need to speak with her but he had no words as yet to explain what had happened. He was still under protection just because of what he had been through but he didn't know how to explain that.

Anna roamed the bedroom that she had been assigned. She turned to study it and then the luxury bathroom. She sighed. Jeremiah had to be involved in something and just that something was, she had no idea. This house was not that of an ordinary abduction. So, what was his story? Anna didn't know.

Early the next morning. Anna crept down the stairs to the front door, her head twisting as she listened for anyone who might be moving around. She could not hear anyone. Anna's hand reached for the lock on the door, twisting it, surprised that there was no sound from it. She crept through the opening, pulling the door closed behind her, just a slight click behind her.

Her feet carried her forward in the darkness. She knew exactly where she was and how close she was to her own home. Her eyes were in constant motion as she searched for anyone who meant her harm.

Standing at her back door thirty minutes later, she hesitated before she reached into her pocket for her keys and unlocked the door. Anna shut it quietly behind her, locking it securely, and then setting the security system. She hesitated before she felt in her pocket, realizing that she didn't have her phone with her. Anna reached to click on a low light in the kitchen before she was through the house, closing the drapes and then stopping in her bedroom. Reaching for clean clothes, Anna showered and then headed for the kitchen. She desperately needed a cup of tea.

Reaching for her mug of tea and her phone, Anna headed for her sun room, feeling the most comfortable and safest there. She could not tell anyone why. It was how it was.

Scrolling through her messages as she sipped at her tea, Anna frowned at the increasingly worried tone of those from her family. She smiled at the one from Haley, just stating that she loved her and was praying for her and would she please stay safe. Anna hesitated at the ones from Joe, knowing that she did have to speak with him. Her fingers hesitated before she sent him a message letting him know that she was at home and would expect to see him in the morning.

Joe reached for his phone which had seemed to be chiming incessantly. He stared at the message from Anna before he thanked God that Anna was safe. He simply responded that he would be there in the morning and that she needed to be ready to speak with him.

Jeremiah rose early in the morning, a frown on his face. He felt something off in the house and dressed quickly before he was running down the oak stairs to find one of his bodyguard heading his way.

"Carl? What is it?" Jeremiah had no idea what had happened.

"It's Anna. She's left the house." Carl was disturbed at that. She should not have been able to walk away but she did. "Peter is heading for her home to see if he can find her."

Jeremiah stared at the man for a moment before his eyes closed. All he could do was pray for his lady and her safety.

"She went home. I have no doubt about that. We should have talked to her last night." Jeremiah was almost angry at that. "Who knows what will happen to her now."

"We know, Jeremiah. We were under orders not to tell her until the boss got here today. You know that." Carl was not backing down from Jeremiah. Instead, he prayed for the man who was fast becoming a friend.

"We should have. The Anna I knew in the past would not have accepted this. She hasn't changed. Now, I don't know if she'll even let me speak with her again." Jeremiah walked away, out of the house and to the truck that he had driven the day before. He had driven away before Carl could stop him.

Chapter 5

Standing in her open doorway that morning, Anna watched as Joe walked towards her. She prayed for words to tell him what happened. She had no idea how to explain what went on. Only God could answer that and at the moment, He was silent.

"Joe?" Anna's soft voice raised Joe's head as he stopped in front of her before he reached to hug her. Anna was a beloved aunt to her nephew's friends and had been for many years.

"You're okay? You weren't hurt?" Joe almost held his breath as he waited for her to respond.

"I'm fine. It was just so strange. It's early, Joe. I'm preparing breakfast for us before I even begin to think to talk to you." Anna stared at him, trying to stare him down and not succeeding at that.

"Just tell me one thing, Anna. Were you hurt in any way?" Joe watched her carefully.

"No, I don't know that I was. Mentally and emotionally? Those are up for debate. I have no idea why I was walked away like that or why I even went." Anna walked away from Joe, heading for the kitchen and the food that she was preparing.

Joe's head dropped for a moment. This was not how this was to go, he decided, but he had to work with Anna. He knew how stubborn that she could be at times. He followed her, reaching to pour their coffee and then placed their utensils on the table.

Anna sat, her eyes on her plate before she looked up at Joe, nodding as he bowed his head to ask a blessing on their food. Joe rose when they finished, cleared away the debris from their meal and refilled their coffee mugs before he sat, his eyes on Anna.

"We need to pray, please, Joe." Anna kept her eyes on her clasped hands. "I don't know what I have just become mixed up in. That is something I will need you to look into. It's complicated."

Joe nodded, having come to that understanding over the last twenty-four hours. He simply bowed his head and prayed for his friend. Raising his head, Joe studied the lady sitting across from him. Anna seemed composed and calm, the only sign of her stress the clenching her hands together tighter and tighter.

"Talk to me, Anna. Tell me what all happened." Joe reached for his notepad and pen, watching her closely.

Anna sighed and nodded, praying for the strength to go through the next while. She began to speak, telling Joe exactly what happened, where she was, and provided a description of the men.

"It was strange, Joe. They didn't harm us. It's almost as if they were protecting Jeremiah. And he didn't say where he had been for so many years. I think that he was waiting for someone to show up before he did that. I just left the house in the night and came home." Anna sighed once more. "And Jeremiah will follow me."

Both of their heads turned as they heard a tap on the front door. Joe was on his feet, heading there and opening the door to find Ardan standing there.

"Ardan?" Joe was not surprised to see the man there. "Come in. Anna is home."

Ardan stared at Joe in shock before he stepped to one side and stared down the hallway.

"She's home? When?" Ardan paused as Joe's hand landed on his arm.

"Sometime early this morning. I have just taken her statement, Ardan. She is not telling everything but what has she has told me is bizarre." Joe walked back to the kitchen, finding Anna on her feet and watching the two men.

Ardan hesitated to approach his sister, a frown on his face as he studied her. Something had happened to her, he decided, and he wanted to know what and who caused it.

"Anna?" Ardan didn't really know what to say to his sister. They were close, closer than a lot of siblings, but in the last few months, Ardan had noticed that Anna was withdrawing from them. When asked about it, she just shrugged and then walked away. To tell the truth, Anna wasn't even sure herself what was going on. She just felt a sense of doom growing around her and could only beg God for protection and peace.

Anna shrugged as she stared back at her brother. She had no words to say what happened. She didn't want Ardan to come done hard on Jeremiah when she herself didn't understand what had happened to him or where he had been.

"Anna? You were with Jeremiah?" Ardan pushed harder, not letting her get away without saying something.

Sighing, Anna finally nodded. She had not wanted to admit that but she didn't seem to have any way around admitting that.

"I was, Ardan. And no, I don't know where he's been for the last length of years. He didn't say. I don't know why he made me go with him." Anna frowned for a moment. "He was met by three men who rushed us away from the parkette near the downtown area and then to a house. Jeremiah seemed to be waiting for someone before he spoke with me. I was not mistreated. It seems as if the men were protecting him, not harming him. That doesn't make a lot of sense."

"It does if they are the ones who found him. I don't think that Jeremiah kept himself away from you just because he wanted to. He was likely kept from returning home, even for all those years. I want to talk with him. What house?" Ardan's voice and face were stern.

"I won't tell you that, Ardan. That's something Joe has to deal with." Anna was on her feet, walking away from the two men, leaving Joe shaking his head at Ardan.

"Let her go for now, Ardan. Support her as she would you. Don't push. You know that she doesn't respond well to being pushed by anyone." Joe was on his feet, walking from the house. He sighed to himself.

This was not what anyone expected, to have Anna disappear, reappear, and then refuse to say what all happened. He had no doubt that what she had said was the truth. He just didn't know if that was all.

31

Anna turned from her computer later that afternoon. She worked from home doing research for authors (and had just sent off what she had found to a friend) and part time in a medical office. On her feet, Anna paced through her house, stopping to stare out of her front door window. She sighed. Jeremiah just had to show up, didn't he? She had no desire to speak with him yet but it didn't look as if she had much option about that.

Opening the door, Anna stood at the top of the steps, watching Jeremiah as he stood at the bottom of the steps. He was worried about her, she could tell.

"Why are you here, Jeremiah? I walked away from you." Anna folded her arms across her abdomen, the sounds of the late afternoon in her ears.

"I need to talk with you, Anna. I didn't want you to leave. It's dangerous for you." Jeremiah took a step up on the stars, stopping as Anna backed away from him. "Anna?"

"I don't know you any more, Jeremiah. I'm not even sure if I can trust you. How do I do this?" Anna blinked back tears that momentarily clouded her eyes. "How do we do this? I need to know why you were gone and what happened. That's not a quick conversation for us to have."

"No, it's not. And I do need to explain to you. You are in danger, Anna, and I don't want any harm to come to you." Jeremiah stepped up to the porch, watching as Anna continued to back away from him. His eyes were pleading with her to let him speak. "Anna?"

"Have a seat, Jeremiah. I'll be right back." Anna walked into the house and returned with two bottles of water, one of which she handed to Jeremiah. She took her seat in her favourite wicker rocker, shuffling the coral and jade cushions around to make herself comfortable. "Ardan knows that you're back. He will be looking for you. And a friend who is a police detective will be tracking you down to speak with you. You need to be honest with us all, Jeremiah. I don't know you any more, like I said, and you don't know me." Anna reached for her necklace, pulling it out from under her T-shirt. A beautiful diamond ring hung from it. "I have worn this for years, grieving your loss and not knowing if you were alive or dead."

"I understand that, Anna. I don't know you either. Not after all this time." Jeremiah drew in a deep breath, praying for his beloved Anna as he did so. "We will talk, Anna. Today is not the day to do so." His hand went up as she opened her mouth to protest. "This involves more than just you and I." Jeremiah's head dropped for a moment before he looked up, regret and some other emotion on his face that she couldn't read. "There are people that need to be involved in that discussion. In case you missed it, I'm still in danger, even more now that I'm home. The three men? They're part of a security detail that I have to have in place for now. Now that I've contacted you, they will move in to protect you. That's not an option, Anna."

<hr>

Anna was on her feet, a look of almost anger on her face.

"You need to leave, Jeremiah. Don't come back until you are ready to tell me exactly where you were and why. This beating around the bush is not getting us anywhere." Anna walked away, not letting Jeremiah see the tears that she could not control. The front door closed quietly behind her and locked under her hand.

Jeremiah had risen when Anna had, dismay and distress on his face. He knew Anna well enough from years ago that she would not back down from him or return to face him that day. He dropped his head for a moment before he simply opened the mail box and dropped in the card that he had picked up for her before he walked down the steps and to his truck. Carl was waiting for him, a look of sympathy on his face.

"Ready to go, Jeremiah?" Carl was watching the area around him, not watching Jeremiah.

"I guess I am, Carl." Jeremiah paused for a moment to stare back at the house, begging God to protect his lady and also to bring quick closure to what he went through. He had lost enough to that man or woman or whoever it was that had locked him away for so many years. "Anna's not ready to hear what I have to say. Only God knows when she will be. I pray that it's soon."

Carl nodded. That was what they were all praying for, he knew, that and protection for both Jeremiah and Anna. They were well aware that someone had been watching Anna over the years and even more so now that Jeremiah had been released and fled back to his home country. It had taken work to get him back, involving the embassy in that country. Now that Jeremiah was home, they needed to solve why he had been locked away in the first place.

"Any thoughts, Jeremiah, as to why?" Carl had had this discussion with his team mates and also with Jeremiah.

"Not really, Carl. I just don't understand it." Jeremiah moved restlessly on the truck seat. "You know what? Can we stop for a burger somewhere? I need that connection with my past life. There is so much rebuilding to do that I'm not sure where to begin."

"We can do that. It will be little steps that move you forward, Jeremiah. For now, we need to keep you out of the public eye as much as possible. We'll work with Anna and her family as best we can." Carl shook his head for a moment. "She's angry and worried, Jeremiah. She also doesn't understand why you disappeared for so long. That's what will be the basis of what you need to discuss with her. I'm not sure how you can do that."

"I know." Jeremiah stared at the man standing near the burger place, a frown on his face. "There's Anna's brother, Ardan."

"It is?" Carl studied the man before his phone was out to take a photo of Ardan. "We need to update the file on the family, Jeremiah. There have been additions to the younger ones."

—

Jeremiah nodded, knowing full well that was the case. He had found the family on social media and studied their photos that were public. He didn't want to reach out to them, not yet, not ready to bring danger to them.

"How long, Carl?" Jeremiah didn't expect an answer. He knew that no one could tell him that. The only one who knew was God and He wasn't sharing that information with Jeremiah.

"You need to heal, Jeremiah. We need to find someone who you can talk to. You'll need counselling."

"I have reached out to someone. I heard of this lady who had an adventure that almost killed her. And then there is someone who works for the Barnabas Foundation. I had reached out to him. He's ready to meet with me whenever I want." Jeremiah blinked back tears. His emotions were all over the place at the moment. That didn't surprise him. He had kept them under such tight control for too many years. Now that he was free at last, his control was relaxing and he knew full well what he would and could expect.

Chapter 7

Anna paced her home late that night. She drew in a deep breath, knowing that at some point she had to speak with her family. And she dreaded that. Anna had no answers for the questions that she knew that they would ask. And not asking the hard questions would not be off the table. That much she knew from her understanding of her family.

The chiming of her phone startled her, causing her to spin, a hand to her mouth to still her scream. What the boys had gone through and now this with Jeremiah had scared her more than she would admit to anyone. Anna crept towards the desk in her office and peeked at the phone. It was Cayce, calling she was sure to ensure that she was okay. She walked away from her phone, not wanting to talk with anyone at that point.

Standing at the living room window, Anna peeked through the drapes. It was what she expected to see. A car was parked at the curb. She just didn't know if it was friend or foe and she was not prepared to march out there and confront whoever it was. Anna finally sought her rest, but that rest was not what she usually experienced. She tossed and turned and finally rose in the very early morning hours to seek her prayer corner. Anna needed that desperately. She frowned as she reached for her Bible. She was troubled that Jeremiah had reappeared and had not told her what had happened. She needed to know why and who had been responsible.

Jeremiah stood on the city sidewalk outside of Anna's home. His feet had brought him there as he escaped from his security team. He was feeling freer in some ways but still a prisoner in other ways. He wanted to be totally free. Jeremiah also wanted to explore what relationship might be remaining with Anna, if there was anything left. She just wasn't cooperating with him. His feet finally took him towards her home where he found a chair to rest in on her front porch. He was not familiar with this home as it was not the home that she had been living in when he disappeared.

Sensing someone around her, Anna cautiously opened her drapes an hour later, letting in the early morning sun. She paused as she stared at the front porch, fear momentarily moving through her. He just had to appear, didn't he?

Anna turned form the window, reluctant to step out onto her front porch, but knowing that at some point she had to. She reached for bottles of juice and then hesitated as her head bowed and she prayed for herself, her family, and for Jeremiah.

Standing in front of Jeremiah, Anna still hesitated to speak. She watched as he looked up at her, taking the bottle of juice that she was extending to him. He shook his head for a moment, not sure how to respond to her.

"You need to talk to me, Jeremiah, and do that today. If not, walk away from me." Anna found her favourite wicker chair and sat. Her eyes did not flicker or waver as she watched him.

"I know that I do, Anna. God help me, I know that I do." Jeremiah's eyes closed for a moment to hide his emotions.

"Then, talk." Anna's own eyes closed as her emotions were beginning to get the better of her.

"I will, Anna. I just need a moment to pray with you and for you. You are in danger now, just because I've been in contact with you. God help me, I've brought more danger to you than you were in." Jeremiah's head bowed as he prayed for his lady as he still thought of her as and begged God for protection for her and for understanding from her. "First, let me tell you that I didn't leave willingly. I was forced to stay away all these years."

"Forced to stay away? Just what do you mean, Jeremiah?" Anna stared at him, shock briefly showing on her face.

"I was forced to stay in that country. I wasn't in prison, even though it felt every day as if it was. You know that I had to go overseas for business for my employer. How I wish that I had simply refused as I had the option to do so." Jeremiah's voice died away for a moment as his thoughts went back in time. It would be hard to relive those years, but he needed to and he needed Anna to understand that he had not voluntarily stayed away from her. "This is going to be hard to say and more importantly, hard for you to hear and understand. Once more, Anna, I didn't stay away from you voluntarily. I was kept away from you, and even now, I don't understand why."

Anna kept her eyes on Jeremiah even as her thoughts raced ahead of what he had said. She had no idea what he was talking about. Her mouth opened and closed a couple of times. Anna prayed for Jeremiah, knowing from the past that he didn't like to hurt people. She just didn't know how he was at this point.

"Continue, Jeremiah. I would really like to know why you disappeared and never returned, not until now. You owe me that much." Anna sat back in her chair, sipping at her bottle of juice before she capped the bottle and set it to one side.

Jeremiah nodded even as he studied the lady in front of him. He had loved and adored her all those years ago and the memories of her had kept him sane through those years.

"I do owe you that, Anna. However, once I have told you what happened, it becomes more dangerous for you. You have been watched over the years by men hired by the man who kept me captive. And kept captive I was. I was not free to leave the building or the small yard that surrounded it for over twenty years, Anna. Do you know what that is like?" Jeremiah's eyes slid closed for a moment as the fear and terror and frustration built up in him once more and he could feel the depression that had been part of his life for so long.

"I don't know how I could, Jeremiah. You walked out of my life with no word. How was I to know that you were held captive?" Anna could feel the anger growing in her even as the sun was rising over the horizon. She prayed for that to be released but knew that it would take a long time.

"I know that, Anna. Please? Let me tell you what happened." Jeremiah's attention turned to the street. Carl and Greg were parked on opposite sides of the street, each watching carefully for anyone who might mean him or Anna harm. They had insisted on that. And someone was in her back yard, he knew, keeping watch that way. "It will take time to tell my story, Anna. And I am so afraid that you will be hurt once more. The man who held me didn't release me voluntarily. Carl and his group came in and rescued me about four months ago. It took time to debrief me and to make arrangements for me to come home once more. Only, I am not sure that this is home any more. My family is gone, not knowing that I was still alive. The man who held me threatened everyone who was connected to me, including Ardan and Bessie and the triplets. Now that the triplets are married and have children, that makes it even more dangerous. He will not hesitate to go after anyone who is close to me." Jeremiah refused to look up, not wanting to see that Anna was rejecting him. He didn't know if he could handle that.   All he could do was pray for his sweetheart as he still thought of her, begging God to protect her and to heal them both.

Anna nodded, having come to that conclusion. She studied the man who now sat in front of her, knowing that he was broken and needed a touch of the Master's hand to heal. She just didn't know if she would be part of that at all.

———

Chapter 8

Jeremiah rubbed at his cheek as he thought back through the years. He had worked as a jeweller for a company in town and would travel every few months to meet with gem dealers or to trade shows. He was the one his employer trusted the most to do that. They were friends from a Bible study at their church. Jeremiah was grateful for the trust shown in him and did his utmost to live up to the expectations that David had in him.

That day so many years ago had started off as normal. Jeremiah had arrived at the gem dealer's business and walked in, waiting for the man to be free. He had walked around the store, noting the jewelry that was on display. He frowned for a moment as he studied one of the necklaces. He recognized it as a stolen piece of jewelry and knew that he had to leave. Only, he never got the chance to do that. Jeremiah had turned to the door only to find an armed guard in front of him to prevent his leaving.

The business man approached Jeremiah, causing Jeremiah to spin to stare at him.

"You have discovered something." The man's voice held a heavy accent as he spoke in English. "That's too bad, Mr. Riley. You cannot leave now that you have discovered that necklace." He nodded at the guard, who reached for Jeremiah and shoved him towards the door that led to the backroom.

Jeremiah struggled to escape the hands that were holding him in place once the door closed behind him.

—

He was unable to. Fear grew in his heart even as he prayed for release. He felt a sharp prick on his arm and twisted to escape it. He was not in time. His body slumped to the floor before he was dragged into a store room and locked in there.

Late that evening, Jeremiah's body was carried from the building and dropped in the man's van. The van was driven hours away from the city and to a compound that the man had in the country. Jeremiah was dragged from the van and to a locked cell. Dumped on the damp ground, he laid still despite the nudges given him by the driver's booted foot. The driver shrugged and walked away, heading back for the city. He knew that his employer would deal with Jeremiah.

The man appeared on the weekend, walking through his compound and studying each of the men and women who were imprisoned there. Some had been there for just weeks, others for years. He stopped in front of Jeremiah's cell, staring through the window at Jeremiah. He knew that Jeremiah was a gifted craftsman and he had been working for months to get Jeremiah into his control. He opened the door, watching as Jeremiah stared at him.

"Mr. Riley? You will work for me from now on. You will never return to your home country. Never again." The man stared at Jeremiah once more before he walked away. He would leave him to think about what he said. He had begun a campaign of destroying Jeremiah's will and power over his own life.

Jeremiah stared at the door, not sure that he had heard the man correctly. Of course, he would go home and soon. His mind was still too fogged from the sedative that he was given the day before to fully understand that the man was correct. He would not go home for years.

Day after day, week after week, month after month, and time that spanned to years saw Jeremiah still a captive. The man had returned multiple times in the beginning to gloat over Jeremiah's plight, simply stating that Jeremiah would eventually agree to work for him. He needed Jeremiah's skills to hide the jewels that he had his men and women steal for him. The only thing was that Jeremiah steadfastly refused to do so. The man could not understand how Jeremiah was refusing to work for him. Everyone always did at some point.

Jeremiah's only request over the years was for a Bible. He was eventually handed one, the employee doing so frowning at Jeremiah. Not one of the employees could understand Jeremiah's refusal to work for the man. Everyone did at some point.

The years dragged slowly for Jeremiah. He spent much time in studying God's Word and in prayer. His thoughts often went to his family and to his sweetheart. Would Anna wait for him for no matter how long it took or would she move on?

Jeremiah steadfastly refused to work for the man. He didn't want to become part of a theft ring and that's exactly what the man ran. He finally gave up on his dream of being free. After twenty years of his life as it was, he knew that no one would find him and that he would die a prisoner.

—

One night, Jeremiah's life changed. He was sound asleep before he felt a hand over his mouth and another hand holding him down on his bunk. His eyes opened in the dim light as fear coursed through his body. He was not prepared to be dragged from his bunk and then through the various doorways and gates to then be shoved into a vehicle. The vehicle took off, no lights showing on it as it sped away from the compound.

Jeremiah shook the hands holding him still off of his arms and turned to the men with him.

"What is going on?" Jeremiah was confused and also angry. He had no idea who these men were, suspecting that they worked for his captor.

"It's okay, Jeremiah Riley. You're a free man now." The man on his right gave a grim smile. "We've finally been able to track you down and free you. We'll get you back to your home town but for now, you need to stay with us."

"I don't understand." Jeremiah was confused. His mind must be playing tricks on him, he decided, or else he was deep in a dream, a recurring dream where he found his freedom.

"You are free, Jeremiah. We're heading for another country that will allow us to debrief you and then get you home. It's not going to be an easy or quick process." Carl, the man sitting on Jeremiah's right, shared a look with Greg, the man on Jeremiah's left. "We'll explain it all but for now, all we can do is ask you to trust us. David sent us."

"David? As in my old employer?" Jeremiah twisted on his seat to study each man in turn. "I thought that he figured I had gone bad."

"No one ever thought that, Jeremiah. You were tracked to that city but the man you were to meet denied that you ever arrived. We were finally able to confirm that a couple of weeks ago. Then we were told where to find you. We moved in to free you as soon as we could." Carl watched with sympathy on his face as Jeremiah took in his words and then rested back against the car seat.

"I don't understand it but God has worked this out, hasn't he?" Jeremiah's eyes closed as he thanked God for his freedom before he slept. The weight of the years was leaving him and he couldn't keep awake.

Chapter 9

Jeremiah walked through the house that he had been brought to, not comfortable with the space or what he felt was luxury after twenty or more years of being in a single rugged cell. Carl watched him closely, knowing that they had to find someone to counsel with him and that might not be possible in the country that they were hiding in at the moment. And hiding they were. The word that had reached them was that the man was furious that Jeremiah had disappeared and that he wanted Jeremiah's life for that.

Carl watched Jeremiah closely over the next few weeks, working with him to try and reacclimatize him back to civilization. He could tell that Jeremiah was fearful when he was out in the town but there wasn't much that could be changed about that. He needed to be out there, to know what civilization was now like. The only thing that Carl hesitated about was telling Jeremiah about his family.

Jeremiah finally turned to Carl one day about two months after he was freed. He wanted to know about his family. But most of all, he wanted to know about Anna.

"Carl? You have not said anything about my family." Jeremiah drew in a deep breath to prepare himself for what he would be told.

"I'm sorry, Jeremiah. Your parents have both passed away. Your mom went just after you disappeared. Your dad about five years later." Carl regretted that they would never know that their son was free, at least not here on earth. He knew of their faith in God and that their trust had been in His freeing of Jeremiah.

Jeremiah nodded. It was what he had expected to hear and had braced himself for that news. He had sensed over time that his parents had gone home.

"Anna?" Jeremiah's voice was barely audible.

Carl gave a brief smile. He had fully been prepared to hear Jeremiah ask about her.

"Anna? She is still in your hometown. She has never married, Jeremiah. No one can tell us if she has ever had another male friend or not. Anna still uses her maiden name." Carl watched with sympathy as Jeremiah's eyes slid closed. "We'll connect you at some point once we get you back there. You two do need to talk."

"What is the talk in town? Do you know what people are saying about me?" Jeremiah was very hesitant to ask, thinking that he would be thought of as a thief and dishonourable man who didn't care about his family.

"They miss you, Jeremiah. We have been in your town and spoken with people who know you. They could not figure out why you disappeared. You are honest in all your dealings, someone who would go out of his way to help anyone who needed it. Your faith in God is what they talk about the most. We have not approached the Koyle family, choosing not to do that. That we will deal with once you're home. You have been missed greatly, Jeremiah. Even today, people are trying to find you and to determine just what happened to you."

"And my captor? He's had people in town, no doubt." Jeremiah blinked back tears. He had not expected to be missed but instead, he expected to have been forgotten.

"He did have before you disappeared. You were watched carefully from what we can determine. David did tell us that the man specifically requested you to come. He didn't think anything of it at the time. No one did until you just never came home. He contacted the man frequently at the time and the man just denied that you ever appeared in his store." Carl was on his feet, moving to the kitchen, and returning with fresh mugs of coffee and a meal for them both. "Eat, Jeremiah. We still have work to do but we'll be heading for your hometown in the next week. Once we're there, we'll keep you separate from the townspeople until you reacclimatize to that town."

Jeremiah nodded, taking the meal without any thought of what he was doing. He ate, his thoughts troubled.

"Anna is okay?" Jeremiah finally looked up at Carl.

"She is. She has gone on to live her life. Her nephews are now grown and each has married with children of their own, the oldest girl about a year now, I think. You should be aware that the three men faced danger when they met their now wives. Those stories are not mine to tell but theirs. And they will tell you, I am sure." Carl rose and gathered up the remnants of their meal. "Rest, Jeremiah. You need to do that. Your body is still recovering from the last twenty years and it has taken a toll on you, whether you realize it or not."

Jeremiah nodded, sitting back in the upholstered chair that he favoured. His eyes closed as he began to pray, begging God for Anna to still be his lady. He sighed. It was in God's hands if she was or not. All he could do was pray for her and then wait on God. He begged God for protection for his lady, knowing that they were both different people than they were when they were young. Anna had always been the only one for him and he for her. Jeremiah didn't know if that was the same now.

Carl stood where he could watch Jeremiah, Greg stopping beside him. They both knew that this was the dangerous part of their mission, getting Jeremiah back to his hometown. They had worked with the embassy in the country they were hiding in to provide documents for Jeremiah. They were ready to leave but hesitated to do so. Word had reached them that the man had men watching the airports in the towns near where they needed to land.

"What's the plan, Carl? Has John said?" Greg spoke of their employer, who was coordinating from their town.

"We're flying into Riverville tomorrow night. From there, we have another security team that will help get us back to Jeremiah's home town. We've worked with Abe Finlay before."

"We have. And with his wife. I suspect Emma is already working on the why's and who." Greg shared a grin with Carl.

"She is. John said that she's forwarding all sorts of information to him and also to the police chief in Jeremiah's town with the stipulation that he tell no one until we have him safe back there." Carl walked away, his phone out to call John. This was a critical point for them, getting Jeremiah safely to the airport and then flying out. "John? We're set from your end?"

"We are, Carl. Be prepared to head out at midnight tonight. We have cleared you to leave no later than that." John gave further instructions that really weren't needed but Carl understood why he was doing that.

"We'll be set to go. Jeremiah's ready to go home. We have resources in place for him to speak with?"

"We do. Get him home safely and we'll go from there. For now, your team stays with him. Abe has stated that he can move his team in if needed or he has two friends with teams that can move in." John hung up abruptly, knowing that Carl needed no further instructions from him and that the longer they were on a call, the greater the chances that Carl and his team would be found.

—

Chapter 10

Jeremiah had settled into his seat on the business class plane, not sure what to expect or how long a trip it would be. He had been awakened two hours previously, hauled to his feet, and then driven to the airport. Carl had simply shaken his head at Jeremiah as that man's mouth opened to ask a question.

"Wait until we're where we need to be, Jeremiah. Then, we'll explain." Carl's hand on Jeremiah's back shoved him towards the door and the car waiting for him.

Two hours later, Carl approached Jeremiah, sitting near him. He sighed to himself. He really needed to speak with Jeremiah and advise him as to what the next steps were. Only, Jeremiah was sleeping and Carl didn't have the heart to awaken him, not at this point.

Jeremiah stirred at last, sensing that something had changed. His eyes opened slowly as he looked around. He wasn't a prisoner any more, he didn't think. He just wasn't sure where he was. Jeremiah jumped as a mug of coffee appeared in his line of sight.

"Jeremiah? You're awake?" Carl's voice held a tinge of amusement in it. "Here. Have your coffee. We need to talk."

"We do, Carl. Where are we?" Jeremiah was refusing to give in and let Carl talk. He was going on the defensive, something that had been expected before this.

"We're in the air, Jeremiah. We're heading home. We'll land in Riverville first and then head by road to a house in your hometown. Your own home is still there, kept updated and maintained. Your parents' will demanded that. They always felt as if you would return home." Carl smiled in sympathy as pain and grief crossed Jeremiah's face. "I'm sorry, Jeremiah, that you missed out on life in your hometown and with your parents and Anna. I'm sorry that you didn't have the family that you should have had to raise and train in God's ways."

"Thank you, Carl. But that's life, isn't it? God has a plan and purpose for me that I just don't see. Do you?" Jeremiah stared down at his mug of coffee. "What can you tell me about what happens next?"

"First, we find you a home to live in. We stay with you. It's okay. It's what we do. John doesn't want to bring in anyone else and disturb where you are in your recovery. He'll rotate us out one or two at a time just so that we can get a break and see our families. Anyone who comes in to replace us will be outside the home. You know our team and that continuity needs to stay."

"I appreciate that. So, how do we get back to my hometown without being seen?" Jeremiah was puzzled at that. "I'm afraid, Carl, I must admit. I don't know that town any more. In fact, I don't know life or civilization any more. He took care of that. I just refused to work with him. I wouldn't be part of his crime. That irked him."

"It did. Your getting away from him? He'll be looking for you to take revenge. We have people watching your lady for you and her family." Carl stood and stared down at Jeremiah. "Catch what sleep you can. We've about eight or nine hours yet in the air before we land to clear customs. And we will clear customs. John is looking after that for us." Carl walked away to head for the cockpit, stopping to stare back at Jeremiah. That man was starting to heal but bringing him back to his hometown and putting him in touch with those who he had loved and left behind would open new wounds and tear the scabs of those wounds that had started to heal.

Jeremiah's head went back on the headrest, his eyes closing. His thoughts were troubled and tumbled over one another. In one way, he was glad to be going home, excited to see his hometown again, and desperate to see Anna. On the other hand, he was deeply afraid to go home and see the hatred and disgust that he was sure would be directed at him. He was also deeply afraid that Anna had indeed moved on, forgotten him, and when he reappeared, would want nothing to do with him. That fear drove him to prayer and begging God for His graciousness in keeping Anna's love alive for him. Then, he was driven to surrender his hopes and dreams to God's will.

Carl hurried down the plane steps, heading for the man waiting for him. He had worked with Abe Finlay and his team at Rebel's Security before. He knew the depth of Abe's faith and how well respected he was in the business even though his team did training now instead of going out on assignments.

"Abe? Good to see you." Carl's hand went out to shake Abe's. "We're all set?"

"We are. John was good to provide us what information that we needed. Let's get him out of here and on his way home. It's been far too long." Abe squinted through the early dawn light. "How is he?"

"His emotions are all over the place, Abe, as you would well expect it to be. He's not sure about being free or being home." Carl turned back to the plane, seeing Greg walking down the stairs with Jeremiah tight behind him. "This is where it gets so dangerous for him."

"It does. We'll get you to your place in his town and then head back here. We're available if you need us as are Richard and Don and their teams. Do not hesitate to call us. And Emma is working on what happened and who all is involved."

"Emma is? Good. I know most people don't know that she's Tracker and what all she does. She'll find what we need if anyone can." Carl pointed towards the SUVs that were waiting, Greg nodding and directing Jeremiah that way. "Thanks for arranging the extra SUV."

"It's what we do, Carl. We've worked together before. Now, let's get on the road. I don't like that we're out here in the open. Who knows if that man has connected us." Abe walked rapidly to the first SUV, closing the door after himself as he sat in the front passenger's seat. "Okay, Luke. Let's head off."

"How is he?" Matt's voice sounded from the back seat.

"He's hurting and angry and disoriented, I would imagine. It's hard being free after over twenty years."

—

Abe could not fathom being held for that long. "I spoke with Darcy last night. She's on board to counsel him if he wants to contact her. She's also working on a profile other than the man who held him captive. She's convinced that someone in his hometown is involved. And no, she doesn't suspect David."

"I can't understand how he got away with that." Luke shook his head even as he headed down the highway, watching the convoy that followed him. "We've got too many vehicles, Abe."

"It seems that way, doesn't it?" Abe was worried about that but knew that one of his own vehicles would break off once they reached that town and head for Anna's home to watch out for her.

"It does, but it's necessary." Matt shifted to stare out of the back window. "He's got a long road ahead of him. What about the lady?"

"The lady? That's an unknown at this point. Carl didn't say much about her but we'll make sure that she's safe for now. After that, it's up to them. John stated that Jeremiah would be put in touch with her in a few weeks. He just doesn't know if Anna will accept Jeremiah back into her life or not."

"That is a good question." Luke shook his head. "I can't image being apart from someone for so long. It was long enough for you and Emma, Abe, those ten years that you were separated."

Abe simply nodded, his thoughts on that time but also on how God had used that time to refine both he and Emma into the people who they were now.

—

Chapter 11

Jeremiah watched with interest as he neared his hometown after way too many years. He saw the growth in it as well as the disrepair of certain businesses. Some businesses and companies were the same but there were many that he just didn't recognize and had no trust that he would ever be able to walk into them a free man. Carl had assured him that he could. Jeremiah had looked at him that day and walked away, his head bent in defeat.

"Jeremiah? We're heading for the other side of town." Carl's hand rested on Jeremiah's arm for a moment. "But before we do that, we will drive by Anna's home, just so that you know she is still alive and well."

Jeremiah nodded, knowing that it was too early in the morning for Anna to be out and about although she had always loved the early morning hours. That he could remember about her.

Greg drove slowly by Anna's home, the other SUVs waiting at the end of the street for him to turn his vehicle and drive back past her house. Jeremiah sat upright, his eyes glued to the house, catching a glimpse of a lady walking down the front steps. It was Anna. He was seeing her for the first time in years. His eyes closed as he tried to control his emotions, unable to do so as tears flowed down his cheeks. The men with him glanced at him and then away, allowing him to grieve in peace. And grieving he was, despite having the confidence that God was in control. He had lost too much time with her for nothing.

Carl shot a look at Jeremiah before he glanced back at the house. He watched as Anna paced to the sidewalk and stood watching the vehicles drive away. They would be back at some point, he knew. Jeremiah would not stay away from Anna. His need to see her was that great.

Jeremiah stretched out on the bed in the room he was assigned. He was exhausted physically but mentally? Emotionally? He was beyond exhaustion. His tears wet the pillow that his head lay on. He could not even form a prayer to thank his Heavenly Father that he was home. He knew that the Holy Spirit would frame that prayer and put into it everything that he would or could want to say. He slept, finally at rest and almost peace, home once more after all those years. He had caught glimpses in the dim light of the town that he had longed to return to. But more importantly, Jeremiah had seen his lady in the dawning light and knew that she was alive and well despite the words that said that she was dead to him.

Abe and his team of seven men drove away from that town, disturbed at what they had been told about Jeremiah. They had exchanged glances with one another before leaving, not sure how to think or even feel about what they had been told. Abe was confident that Emma would work on this investigation as quickly as she could. He just didn't know how quickly that she would be able to find the information and pass it on to someone on that town's police force who would believe her or even believe Jeremiah. His story was just too bizarre but Abe had seen similar events and imprisonments and had helped more than once to free the victim.

Late that afternoon, Jeremiah rose and then reached for clean clothes. He finally was at home, he decided, even though it wasn't his own home. He had seen his lady but not to talk to. Carl had promised him that would happen. First, Jeremiah needed to speak with someone on the police force. Carl and Greg had reached out to John who had reached out to the police chief. The police chief had then reached out to the head of his detective squad to determine who had the lower case load and would be the best to speak with Jeremiah when the time was right. That lot had fallen to Joe, unbeknownst to John that he was a good friend of the Koyle brothers. God was placing people where He wanted and needed them. It had happened before and would continue to happen. They were all aware of that.

Joe had taken the file folder handed to him with instructions not to read it as yet. He would be told when he would be able to access that. This was an unusual move but he nodded, setting it carefully into a desk drawer. He would open the drawer each day, stare at the folder, and then close the drawer. The time was not yet ready for him to read it and then move forward with his investigation. Joe sensed that it would be life changing for many involved in it. He just didn't realize the danger that would come with that investigation.

Jeremiah walked slowly down the stairs that afternoon, seeking for answers that weren't forthcoming. Carl had simply shaken his head at

———

Jeremiah and pointed to the kitchen. Jeremiah sighed. He was home but still not free. He begged God for freedom and to see his lady. God was not allowing that as yet. Jeremiah surrendered his will to his Father's will and then turned to walk away from the kitchen. He needed to find a prayer corner and do it right then.

Carl followed Jeremiah to where the other man finally sat. He set a bottle of water beside him and a Bible and then walked away, knowing that Jeremiah needed that time alone.

Greg turned from where he was working on a meal for them all, knowing that the men would take turns coming in to eat. He glanced past Carl towards the hallway.

"Where's Jeremiah?"

"He found a chair for a prayer corner, I suspect. He's hurting in so many ways, Greg. I have no idea how to help him other than to pray for him." Carl was simply stating the truth that they were all feeling. "When do you go home?"

"Tomorrow for a week. John wants one of us with Jeremiah while the other one is away. Jeremiah knows the other men but you and I have been closest to him."

"We have been." Carl poured their coffee and then leant back against the counter. "I'm off the next week. It's going to be difficult to keep him away from Anna. Now that he's home and has seen her, he'll want to head that way."

"He will and we can't let him." Greg turned back to face Carl. "Do we know who the investigator will be?"

"We do. A young man by the name of Joe. The thing of it is? He's friends with the Koyle brothers and was the investigator for what they went through." Carl rubbed at the back of his neck, his eyes on the hallway. "I don't know if Jeremiah is familiar with that investigator or not."

"Not likely. He may not remember him after so many years." Greg set the plates on the table and then walked away to find Jeremiah, returning with the older man. "We need to eat, Jeremiah, and then you need to rest again. We'll get you to see Anna at some point in the next week or two. For now, we need to keep you here and away from her. I can guarantee you that someone is watching Anna closely and has been since you disappeared. Her family will be watched as well."

Jeremiah nodded, knowing that Greg was speaking the truth. He ate what he could of the stew and then excusing himself, he headed back for his bedroom. Jeremiah could hardly hold his eyes open as he sank down on the bed and pulled the covers over himself. All he could do before he slept was to beg God for protection for Anna and her family.

Chapter 12

Coming back to the present day, Jeremiah rubbed at his cheek, not willing to look up at Anna. He had heard soft sounds from her as he told her his story.

Anna's hand covered her mouth even as she swiped at the tears that flowed down her cheeks. She had no idea that Jeremiah had been held a captive all those years. Her thoughts had been that he had moved on from their town and from her and had found a new lady to love.

"Jeremiah?" Anna's voice was broken and soft. She was on her knees beside him to hug him before moving back to her seat.

Jeremiah looked up at Anna, seeing the devastation on her face. He didn't move from his seat, knowing that he couldn't and that he had to let her have this time. He had had many years to accept his fate. She was just learning about what had kept them apart.

"I need to think over this, Jeremiah." She looked up as she heard footsteps approaching the porch. "Just who are you?"

Carl grinned at Anna for a moment as Jeremiah rose to his feet.

"This is Carl, Anna. He is one of the men who found me and has been helping me. Memorize his face. You may need his help in the future." Jeremiah hesitated beside Anna before he laid a hand on her shoulder and then walked down the stairs, knowing that his time with her was over for the day.

"We'll look after him as best that we can, Anna." Carl extended a business card to her. "Memorize this number and then destroy the card. This will put you in touch with John, our employer. He can reach us at any time if you need us." He bit at his lip for a moment, showing his hesitation. "And I suspect that you will need us at some point." He walked away after Jeremiah, leaving Anna staring after them before she stared down at the card.

Three hours later, Ardan stood in front of his sister. He had tracked her down in her back yard.

"Anna? What is going on? You disappeared and now you're home again." Ardan's hands rose in the air as he waved them at her.

"I did and I am home again. I can't tell you what all happened, Ardan. Someone else is involved and their safety takes precedence over anything that I could say." Anna had a look on her face that pleaded with her brother to understand.

"I don't understand, Anna. Who is it?" Ardan drew in a deep breath. "Jeremiah! It has to be him. You would be willing to speak if he wasn't involved."

Anna turned away from Ardan. She didn't want him to see the acceptance on her face that he had guessed correctly. She just couldn't put anyone else at risk. It was difficult enough to not tell him. They had few secrets from one another. The biggest one had been her engagement to Jeremiah. They had become engaged just a few days before he had to travel overseas and they had agreed not to tell anyone until he was home and they could do that together. That had

—

seemed the best decision at the time. Anna had honoured their agreement as much as she had wanted to tell his parents.

"Anna? Are you in danger?" Ardan's hands rested on his sister's shoulders.

"I am, I think, Ardan. And I don't know who from. Apparently, I've been in danger for years without knowing why or from whom." Anna drew in a deep breath, seeing the rest of her family now standing in front of her. "I'm sorry. I can't tell you why or who. I don't know and no one seems able to tell me."

"That's okay, Anna. We'll be careful. You need to be that watchful as well." Bessie simply hugged her beloved sister-in-law. "What can we do until you can tell us?"

"I have no idea." Anna's eyes closed against the tears that she would refuse to shed until she was on her own. Knowing her family, she would not be alone for hours.

"Well, then, we just make plans. The boys and their wives can help." Bessie drew Anna into her office and shoved her into a chair. She looked around, seeing that they were on their own. "You don't have to say, Anna, but Jeremiah must be back in town after all these years. That is the only thing that I can think of that would make you so fearful and withdrawn from us." She didn't wait for any answer, instead reaching for a pen and a pad of paper. "We need to go back to when you two were dating and see what you can remember about what danger he might have been in."

—

"I don't know that I can remember what happened that long ago, Bessie. From what I can remember, he was not in any danger. He did have to travel but that was part of his work. We accepted that. He just left and never came back. I didn't understand that nor did his parents. They waited for him to come home only Jeremiah just didn't do that." Anna didn't see the men in her family standing just outside of the office door, listening to the conversation.

"What about his employer? I don't remember any rumours about him." Bessie scowled at the pen that she was holding.

"He was never into any criminal activities. That was looked at when Jeremiah didn't come home. As far as I know, his disappearance is still an open case." Anna looked up at Bessie. "I can't say what happened to him, Anna. I don't know."

"We understand that, Anna. It's just that we need to start somewhere to figure out what happened to you." Bessie's eyes were on Anna. She caught the subtle shift in Anna's facial expressions and nodded. Jeremiah's back home, she decided, and Anna has seen him. That's where she was when she disappeared. Bessie looked up and shared a look with Ardan who nodded in response.

The triplets stared between the three older adults, feeling the undercurrents that were flowing from them, but unsettled as to why. They looked at one another and then at their wives who were nodding at them. The younger adults moved away, Arlyn barely waiting until they were out of earshot.

"What was that all about?" Arlyn stared behind him towards the office.

"I would think that Jeremiah has suddenly reappeared." Cayce hugged Haley. "That's where Aunt Anna had disappeared to. She's seen him."

"And she's keeping quiet to protect him and herself." Briar nodded at the others. 'We need to reach out to our friends. I wonder if Joe is involved."

"He won't say at first, you know." Skylor spoke up at last, reaching to gather her daughter close. "And that means Anna is in danger right now."

Chapter 13

Ardan stared at Bessie late that same afternoon, his head shaking in the negative.

"There is no way that Jeremiah is back. Or that Anna has seen him." Ardan was certain of that.

"She's not going to say, Ardan. Not until it's safe." Bessie threw up her hands in frustration before she walked away to their sunroom, finding her favourite rocker. She heard footsteps following her, Ardan appearing right behind her.

"I don't get it, Bessie. How do you know? I would think that I would know if my own sister had seen him." Ardan found a seat, leaning forward to watch his wife's face.

"There was something on her face this morning when you two were talking. It was only a brief glimpse on her face that I caught. She's seen him and is trying to figure out how to get to know him again. I suspect that she is in danger as well." Bessie sighed, her hand reaching for Ardan's. "We need to pray for her. I think that when she disappeared, she was with him."

"That's possible, I guess. I thought that he was either dead or moved on." Ardan sat back, his eyes raising as he heard footsteps walking their way and their sons appeared. "Boys?"

"We need to start looking into this, Dad." Arlyn spoke for the group. "What can you tell us?"

"About what?" Ardan studied his three boys, wishing that this was different. It seemed that his sister was now involved in something dangerous that she was not willing to talk to him about.

"About Aunt Anna. About Jeremiah. We need to do this, Dad." Briar spoke up. "What do you know about him?"

Ardan simply shook his head and rose, walking away from his family. His emotions were raw at this point. Cayce watched him walk away and then followed him, finding a seat beside him on the back patio.

"Cayce? You want to do this?" Ardan finally spoke to his son.

"We all do, Dad. Aunt Anna was there for us when we went through what we did. We don't want to see her hurt any more than she has been."

"She has kept it all quiet and bottled up. That's just who she is." Ardan nodded at last. "When are you thinking of working on this?"

"Tomorrow. It's Saturday. Where do you want to work?" Cayce didn't push his father, knowing that Ardan would speak when he was ready.

Ardan finally nodded. They needed to do this.

"Reach out to whoever it is that you need to. We can't do this on our own." Ardan's eyes closed as he prayed for his sister. She was in danger, he had no doubt about that.

Standing at her back door late that night, Anna watched the activity in her back yard. She had no

—

lights on and the only illumination in the back yard was from the moon, stars, and her solar lights. She frowned. It wasn't those men who were keeping Jeremiah safe. She had no idea who they were. Seeking her rest once the men disappeared, Anna slept but was on her feet early in the morning. She sought her back yard, finding the cameras that had been planted there. She simply pulled them from their hiding places and boxed them up. At some point, an investigator would be assigned to Jeremiah and she would turn them over at that point.

Jeremiah walked back through the house that he was living in. He wanted to go home, to his own home, but was told that wasn't possible. He was getting frustrated and angry that he still felt like a prisoner. He looked around, feeling in his pocket for a set of keys that he had kept hidden for years, and then simply walking out of the house. He didn't realize the consternation that happened in that very house thirty minutes after he left.

Carl ran for his car, heading for Anna. That lady stared at him in shock before she shook her head.

"I haven't seen him, Carl. Not since yesterday when he was here." Anna rubbed at her arms, not sure what to say. "Have you looked for him?"

"We are, Anna, but we just don't know where he would be." Carl was frustrated as he walked away. He had no idea of where to look for Jeremiah. They needed to regroup as a team and find him. The word that was reaching them was that the man was back in town and looking for Jeremiah.

—

Anna stared after Carl as he walked away. She could see the frustration and concern that he felt just in how he was moving. All she could do at the present was pray for Jeremiah and for his safety. She was due at work in the medical office that employed her.

That afternoon, Anna's car slowed in front of the old Riley home. She shoved the car into park and then turned off the ignition. The house had been maintained since the elder Rileys had passed away. She drove by it every few months. Today was different. Today, Anna was looking for Jeremiah and she felt certain that he was here.

Anna's head bowed as she prayed for her friend. She had no idea where they stood with one another. They needed to get to know one another again. There was no guarantee that they would ever be a couple again. Anna's fingers found the ring that she still had on the necklace.

Walking around the house, Anna searched for any sign that Jeremiah was there. There were subtle signs that he was. She didn't want to put him in any more danger that he was already in. Her feet carried her up the back steps and onto the wraparound porch. She hesitated for a moment before she reached for the knob on the back door. It twisted under her hand. Anna hesitated for a moment before she shoved the door open and then stepped inside. Memories flooded her mind as she stood in the kitchen. She had spent many hours there with Jeremiah over the years.

Spinning as she heard a slight noise, Anna's hand covered her mouth to stifle her scream. Her eyes were huge as she stared at the man who stopped in the doorway. Jeremiah was there, she discovered, watching her closely.

"Anna? Why are you here?" Jeremiah didn't move towards her. He was afraid for her. He found letters piling up in the mailbox that threatened her and her family. "You need to stay away from me."

"Jeremiah? Do you know that Carl is looking for you? What did you do?" Anna stared at him, still in shock that he was standing there.

"I know, Anna. I know that he is. I felt stifled and confined. I have had enough of that." Jeremiah walked towards her, his hands raising and dropping before he gently laid them on her shoulders. "You shouldn't be here."

"I had to find you, Jeremiah. We still need to talk." Anna stepped backwards. "Are you ready to talk yet?"

Jeremiah stared at her and shook his head. He was not ready yet to speak with her but that time was fast approaching."

———

Chapter 14

Anna turned to the counter, staring at the few appliances that were there. Jeremiah had found the newer ones that his mother had purchased. He just wasn't sure how to use them.

"Jeremiah? What are you doing here?" Anna turned back to him.

"Trying to get my life back, if I can." Jeremiah sighed, frustration evident on his face. "I know, Anna. I know. I won't have my old life back. I have to get used to a new normal. God is here with me and protected me over the years. That doesn't mean that I have to like what happened." Anger sparked briefly on his face before he drew a neutral look back over it. "And just what are you doing here? Do you not understand how dangerous it is for you?"

Anna stared at him, not sure what to say or think. She shook her head for a moment before her mouth opened and closed. She knew how dangerous it was. He didn't have to tell her that.

"I know how dangerous it is, Jeremiah. The triplets went through danger when they met their now wives. Briar was forced to marry Brynne. So don't tell how dangerous it is to come back into your life." Anger sparked on Anna's face. "Now, what are you planning on doing?"

Jeremiah shrugged. He had no idea that had happened to the boys. No one had explained that to him. He sighed, his anger waning.

"I just don't want to see you hurt, Anna. If you are around me, you will be." He stared at Anna as she snorted. "Anna?"

"Don't you get it, Jeremiah? It doesn't matter if I walk away. We have been seen together. You know that they have been watching me and the family. So, what are your plans?" Anna refused to back down from him.

"You do need to stay away from me, Anna. I don't want to see you hurt." Jeremiah turned away from Anna for a moment and then heard the back door clicked closed. He spun around and then almost ran for the front door. He watched as Anna drove away. Jeremiah's head dropped for a moment. He had succeeded in chasing Anna away from him, not that he wanted to. He wanted to rekindle his friendship with her. His memories of Anna had been what had kept him sane over all the years and he needed to cling to those. Jeremiah was just so afraid for Anna, knowing the character of the man who had held him captive all those years.

Anna drove away, hardly able to see for the tears that clouded her eyes. She had not expected Jeremiah to react as he had. She had forgotten how long that he had been gone and what he had likely experienced. She parked at her work place, not wanting to go into the medical office before she looked at her phone. Anna sighed. Her mind must be confused, she decided. It was Saturday and she didn't work on Saturdays. Just what would she get up to today? Anna jumped as her phone chimed, throwing it onto the passenger's seat before she retrieved it. It was Arlyn, just wanting to meet her for coffee. Would she do that for him? She sent off a quick reply before driving away, heading for their favourite diner. Anna did not notice the car that was following her, the driver looking for an opportunity to stop her car and take her away from Jeremiah. That just didn't happen.

Anna parked in her garage, the door closing behind her. To say that she was disturbed was an understatement. She walked rapidly through her home to the office where she sat at her desk. Her head dropped for a moment as she contemplated what was going on. Anna was troubled and sad. Jeremiah was in danger still and it seemed as if that that danger was not approaching here. She could not go to anyone, she thought.

The pealing of the doorbell startled her. Anna was on her feet, a hand to her throat, before she crept to the front door and peeked out. Joe stood there. Anna sighed. Now, what did he want?

Opening the door, Anna studied Joe and then the car parked across the street from her home. She frowned. Greg was there. Anna sighed to herself. Of course, he would be there. He needed to let her alone and leave her be.

"Anna?" Joe's voice brought her attention back to him. "May I come in? We need to speak."

"We do." Anna stepped back before she headed for the kitchen. "Have you had your lunch yet?"

"No, I haven't. Thanks, Anna." Joe followed Anna to a kitchen that was almost as familiar as that of his parents. "Let me help you."

———

Joe studied Anna as they prepared a simple meal and then ate it. Clearing away the debris from their meal, he refilled their coffee cups and then sat before his head was bowed to pray for the lady who was almost an aunt to him, he was that close to her.

Raising her head, Anna studied her young friend. He had been around all his life, just because of his friendship with the triplets. And then too, he had been the investigators in what those three boys had gone through.

"Anna? What's going on?" Joe reached for his briefcase, pulling out a file folder that he set on the tabletop. "Where is Jeremiah?"

"You know?" At his nod, Anna sighed. She was not prepared to put Jeremiah at any more risk than he was already at. "I won't tell you, Joe. Not without his permission. But for now, I would say that he is safe."

"Is he? Is he really?" Joe didn't back down from Anna, something that was unusual for him. "He is at a great risk of being killed, Anna, being back in his home town. And because you are linked to him, you are at risk."

"I understand that, Joe. I really do understand that." Anna stared past him. "I have spoken with him on a few occasions over the past few days. I know what he faced over the years. God protected him and will protect him despite the best efforts of those against him. If it means his death, he has accepted that fact over the years."

Joe was nodding as she spoke. He had finally read through the paperwork that had been provided to him. He was amazed that Jeremiah had survived but also that he had been able to escape. He didn't know who the men were that had rescued the older man. They were not named in his paperwork.

"Talk to me, Anna. You need to. I'm the investigator on this. I know that you disappeared for a while that day. Were you with Jeremiah?" Joe watched with compassion as various emotions flickered across Anna's face. This was unusual for her. She usually kept her emotions from her face, except when her nephews had been through their adventures as they were called.

Anna finally looked up and nodded. She had to speak with Joe. She just didn't want to. This is where she needed to rely on her Heavenly Father to speak for her.

Chapter 15

Anna hesitated to speak. If she did open up to Joe, it would put Jeremiah in more danger, she decided. She looked at the young man, seeing the compassion on his face.

"What do you remember about Jeremiah?" Anna's question caught Joe off guard for a moment.

"Jeremiah? Not a lot. I can remember him being around with you, playing with the triplets and me. He was a kind compassionate man who was never too busy for us. Why do you ask that?" Joe was puzzled at the question that Anna had asked him.

"I need to know what you remember about him. What you do remember will colour how you react with him now. I know. I know. You are a police investigator and need to keep your personal feelings to one side. In this case? I don't know if you can. Can you?" Anna was challenging him and Joe knew that.

"I can try, Anna. It's hard sometimes to keep personal feelings separate from those of an investigator. Cases get to us over the course of the investigation. This?" He held up the file folder. "This is what I was given and only allowed to read last night. It is an interesting read, Anna. We need to discuss it."

Anna looked around as she heard a soft tap at the front door and sighed. This was not what she wanted that day. She wanted to be on her own and try to work through her feelings and what was going on. On her

---

feet, Anna paced to the front door, to stare at Jeremiah as he stood there.

"What are you doing here?" Anna stepped backwards as Jeremiah moved towards her. "You should not be here." Anna heard soft footsteps behind her and sighed. Joe just had to come to see what was the matter. "Jeremiah, you may remember Joe from when he was young. He's the investigator on your case. You may as well come in and speak with him now that you're here." She stalked away, heading for her office, quietly shutting the door behind her.

Jeremiah stared after her, his mouth slightly open, shocked that she had simply walked away. He heard a soft chuckle from Joe and spun to stare at him.

"She does that, Jeremiah, if I may call you that. We are acquainted. Anna has taken to walking away if she's upset or thinking through something. This is something new for her and developed when the triplets were going through their struggles." Joe pointed towards the kitchen. "Come and sit. We do need to talk. I have been given a file folder of information that I need to verify with you."

Jeremiah sighed, knowing that was the truth that Joe was speaking. He just didn't want to do that. He wanted to find Anna instead. He was afraid for her, not sure if she was still his lady, but because she had been in their past, she was in danger. Carl had tracked him down and reinforced that view.

"We do need to talk, Joe. I do remember you. You're a lot more grown up since the last time that I saw you." Jeremiah was pulling out a chair to sit and didn't see the grin that crossed Joe's face. "Where do we start?"

"Tell me what happened, what you feel, what you think, what you want." Joe sat, his pen poised over his notepad. "Don't hold back anything, Jeremiah. Nothing really shocks me any more."

"I can understand that to a certain degree." Jeremiah rubbed his hand along the dark oak table. "I don't know where to start, Joe." He sighed and then just began to talk, Joe making his notes as he went along. Joe knew that he would be going back over his notes and questioning Jeremiah many times on what he was saying.

"So, this man? You knew him from before?" Joe watched Jeremiah's reaction to the question.

"No, I can't say that I did. I was asked to go over there and meet with him. He had some jewels that we were interested in. David felt that I was the best one to go even though I was the youngest of us all. He had no idea of what awaited me. I have talked to him on the phone. He was devastated to hear what had happened." Jeremiah looked up at that point, finding Joe focusing on him. "Why?"

"Why? Why take you captive and keep you that way for years?" At Jeremiah's nod, Joe sighed. He just had to ask that question, didn't he? He prayed for words, not sure what to say. "It appears that he wanted you to work for him, designing new jewelry from stolen jewelry. I would say that you refused."

Jeremiah nodded. Joe had confirmed his thoughts. That was what David had indicated that his feelings were as well. He had had someone search out the man and found that he was a career criminal, hiding behind his store.

"David has looked into him further. What we were able to find twenty-some years ago was not the truth. That man is a career criminal and thief. I wish that I had known that at the time. We would never have met with him and then had me disappear for so many years. Those years I will never get back." Jeremiah blinked hard to control his emotions. "I lost all that time with Anna, and I don't know where we stand now as a couple. We will likely walk away from one another."

"God was there with you, Jeremiah. You spent all those years in studying His Word and prayer. That enforced quiet has changed you. You could have become bitter and walked away from God. You didn't. You chose to let God work in your life. I would suspect that you were a witness for Him where you were and that witness will have borne fruit for him."

Jeremiah thought through that and then nodded. He had been able to witness to the others, although he kept as quiet as he could. If the guards had found out that he had done that, he was isolated for days, if not weeks. He gradually just talked quietly among the men, knowing that someone would tell on him. But he was surprised that no one did. They listened to him and then walked away.

"It's true, Joe. I did suffer at first for being that witness but over time, the guards and the prisoners just listened and then walked away. I have no idea how many I reached. Only God knows that." Jeremiah rubbed at his cheek. "I worried about Anna all that time. I didn't know if they would go after her or not."

"There has been someone watching her over the years. We have verified that. Don't ask how, please. That is part of our investigation." Joe shuffled through his notes and then the paperwork in the folder. "What do we do with you, Jeremiah? You're at risk here. They'll go after you to seek revenge. You're the first one, we think, to have gotten away from him. I have spoken with John." Joe watched as Jeremiah's head jerked upright. "Yes, we have spoken. He can't leave his team with you much longer. That's a worry, Jeremiah. How do we keep you safe and keep Anna safe as well? I know that you won't walk away from her, not until you arc satisfied that there is no relationship between you two and that she is safe."

"That's true, Joe. I can't walk away from her. But I do need to be out and about in my town. I need to familiarize myself with my town again and reach out to those who had been friends. Anna and her family are the first ones that I want to do that with."

"We understand, but you need to understand. Arlyn, Briar, and Cayce went through some real difficulties when they met the ladies who are now their wives. They have young children that we need to watch out for. None of us want to see them hurt or to disappear. And that's what that man will do." Joe was stern with Jeremiah.

Jeremiah nodded. He was well aware of the character of the man who had imprisoned him. He feared for Anna and her family but he was driven to be near her. He had never stopped loving her and dreaming of some day being free to marry her as their plans had been. He just didn't know if that would ever happen now. Too many years had gone by and they both had grown and changed. Only God would allow them to move forward. All he could do was pray for His protection on them. He prayed for them to be hidden in the hollow of the rock and covered with His hand.

Chapter 16

Anna had walked towards the kitchen, listening to the quiet conversation between the two men. She drew in a deep breath, her arms wrapped around herself. She had no idea that was how Jeremiah felt. She wanted to get to know her friend again but as he had stated, life and circumstances had changed her and changed him as well. They were back at the beginning of a friendship. Anna had no doubt what they both wanted but she had no confidence that they would move forward as a couple. All she could do was pray for them both and then for the investigators. There was more than one, she knew. An investigator from the country overseas had been in touch with her early that morning. Anna had not been able to provide much information for him other than to beg him to solve the investigation and let Jeremiah go on with his life.

Jeremiah sensed that Anna was nearby and was on his feet, despite Joe's protest to the contrary. He paused in front of her before he held out his hands, finding Anna's hesitation to take his not alarming or worrisome. Anna finally reached for his hands, finding Jeremiah's grasp strong but not too tight.

"Anna? Can you join us?" Jeremiah waited patiently for her to respond.

Anna finally nodded, walking past Jeremiah to where Joe had stood to await for her. She shook her head at him, not wanting to speak with him but knowing that she didn't have much choice. Seating herself at the table, Anna folded her hands together, a prayer for protection and understanding rising within her. She knew that God was there and was protecting her and Jeremiah and yes, her family as well.

"Joe? What is it that you want to talk to me about?"

"Anna? I know you. You are worried about your family. That reflects in how you are reacting to Jeremiah and to the investigation. We need you to cooperate with us. There is no option for you to do anything but that." Joe's voice was stern, sterner than he wanted to be, but he knew that he had to be. She would accept nothing else.

"I know, Joe. I know. I have to hear what you have to say. I just don't want to." Anna's face dropped for a moment as she struggled to understand what she was now involved in. "Where is God in all this? Where has He been for the last 20 plus years?"

"Right here, Anna. We don't know why He has allowed this, and that is exactly what He has done. He could have prevented Jeremiah from going overseas. He could have prevented Jeremiah being locked away for all those years. He has a plan and purpose for all this. Jeremiah has reached out to witness for Him in ways that we will never understand here on earth. The same with you, Anna. I have heard of your witness over the last day or so. I don't know if you realize how you have reached others. God has worked through both of you. He has kept you safe, covering you with His hand in the cleft of that rock. He has led to John and his team finding Jeremiah and bringing him home. We still have a lot of leg work to do to solve this and to bring that man to justice. It also involves contact with another government. That complicates everything.”

“I know, Joe. I know that.” Anna stared at Jeremiah, seeing the impassive look on his face. “Jeremiah?”

“Anna? Joe is correct. We do need to work together on this. I just don’t know how safe that will be.” Jeremiah refused to look at Joe who was nodding at his words. “We’ll talk over and over, Anna.” Jeremiah was on his feet, moving from the room, the front door clicking quietly behind him.

Anna stared after him, knowing that he had to walk away but sorrowful that he felt that he had to. Joe shook his head, not sure what to say.

“Anna? You have never said over the years. How close were you two?” Joe waited somewhat impatiently for Anna to respond.

Anna turned to stare at him, knowing that he would probe until he had the answers. She reached for her necklace, pulling it out from under her T-shirt and held it up. The sunlight reflected off the diamond in the ring.

“This close, Joe. We became engaged just two days before he had to leave on that trip. We were keeping it quiet until he returned. At that point, we planned to give a dinner and tell our families. Only that never happened. He didn’t come back. Now that he’s back? I have no idea where we stand. We’re strangers to one another. If we do go on with the engagement, we need to learn about one another again. We need to get to know one another. This has changed

---

all that. Right now? Neither one of us is sure that we do want what we promised at one time. Can you tell me if that will happen?"

Joe shook his head. The only one who could tell her that was God. It was in His timing and in His will. He gathered up his paperwork at last and walked away, not satisfied that he had accomplished anything. He also feared for Anna and Jeremiah. He knew that danger was approaching them. The word on the street was that Anna and Jeremiah were facing danger and perhaps even death.

Skylor, Brynne and Haley stood in Anna's kitchen two hours later. They had come to find their aunt by marriage. Their children were with their fathers, who were delighted to watch their own children.

"Aunt Anna?" Skylor reached to hug Anna. "What has happened? Something has."

"It has. Jeremiah has been around and spoken with both Joe and myself." Anna sighed. "We need to meet as a family, Skylor. I'm just not sure how to say what I need to. And I don't want anyone to look down on Jeremiah. It was not his fault. He was held captive for over twenty years, prevented from leaving that country." Anna looked around at the three young ladies. "So, where do we meet?"

"Here. We'll do a potluck, Aunt Anna." Haley reached to hug Anna. "I'll send out a group text and we'll work on something here."

Anna nodded before she walked away to find quiet and solace. She needed that time alone and then to spend time with her Heavenly Father. She was worried about Jeremiah but also concerned about her family. They would be in danger, she thought, just because of what she was facing even though Anna had no idea what she was exactly facing.

The three younger ladies watched as she walked away from them before they shared a look. They had reached out to Bessie who appeared shortly afterwards, a question on her face. They just hugged one another and then worked on their meal. The four men appeared shortly, surprise on their faces that they were meeting with Anna.

Ardan walked away from the group, heading for where he thought he would find his sister. He stood for a moment in the sunroom door, watching her before he walked over and sat near her. His heart was hurting for his sister and all he could do at the present was pray for her.

Anna's eyes found her brother sitting near her, his own eyes watching his beloved younger sister.

"Anna? Are you okay?" Ardan kept his voice low. He could hear the laughter from the kitchen but his focus was solely on his sister. He looked around at the comfortable room with its soft peach walls, dark flooring and comfortable seating. It was just so his sister.

Anna shrugged before she spoke, pouring out all that had happened in the last few days. Ardan was not surprised to hear that Jeremiah had met with her. What disturbed him was the danger that it seemed Anna was now facing.

Chapter 17

Anna turned from locking her door after her family that night. She didn't think that they were really any further ahead in what they were looking at. She headed for her kitchen, seeing that it was tidy for the night. Anna then reached for a new cup of tea and then for her back porch. It was still warm even though night had fallen.

Sitting in her favourite rocker, Anna set her cup on the table beside her. She refused to think about what had happened, focusing on the verses that she could remember about protection and safety. She knew that God was in control and that He didn't want anything but His best for her. Unfortunately, His will sometimes allowed danger into their lives. She recognized and accepted that, having seen her nephews go through danger and knew that many of their friends had faced the same. She just didn't think that it would ever affect her in this way. Anna's head went back on the chair as her eyes slid closed. She had not wept when Jeremiah had disappeared, at least not outwardly. Tonight? Anna wept for what she had lost. She wept for the love of her life, Jeremiah, knowing that their relationship had changed. Anna grieved the lost years and the changes in Jeremiah. She placed her life once more into her Father's hands, knowing that she was walking through some very deep and dark valleys in her life, more than she had ever faced before.

Anna didn't hear the footsteps that approached her deck and then paused. The man hadn't realized that she was out on the deck until he saw her. He looked down at the package in his hands that he needed to leave for her. He retreated and moved instead to her front porch, leaving the package at her door and then walking away. He was troubled. He had really wanted to speak with her but now wasn't the time.

Rising at last, Anna headed into her house, locking the door behind her. She felt bereft that night, looking back over her life. She had no idea if she had done the right thing, waiting for Jeremiah to return. Anna could only leave the pieces of her life in God's hands, knowing that He only wanted the best for her.

Jeremiah stood at the living room window of his childhood home. He had refused Carl's offer of someone to stay with him. He wanted the solitude that being alone meant. Jeremiah had spent the time alone in prayer and supplication, begging God to protect his lady. He had then become silent before his Father, just waiting for the peace and comfort that only God could give.

The next morning, Joe walked towards Anna's home, having more questions for her. He paused as he stepped up onto the porch, his eyes on the package sitting there. His finger reached for the door bell even as his head tilted to study the writing on the package, simply Anna's name.

Anna stood in the open doorway, her eyes on Joe before they dropped to the package. Before Joe could stop her, she had reached for the package and disappeared back into the house. Joe sighed before he stepped inside and closed the door behind him, walking through the house after Anna.

—

"Anna? Don't open that." Joe's hand reached too late to stop her.

Anna opened the package carefully, not having any fear about it. She stared down at the papers that lay inside the box before she had pulled them out. Anna ignored Joe's comment that she needed to wait for him to look them over.

"It's addressed to me, Joe." Anna looked up at Joe, seeing the frown on his face. "I won't give them to you. And just why are you here?"

"I needed to speak with you again." Joe was frustrated. Anna just wasn't letting him see the papers. "What are those papers, Anna?"

"I have no idea, Joe. I need to go over them. If you need anything from them, I will let you have that. For now? Unless you have your questions ready, I think that you need to leave." Anna walked away from Joe.

Joe stared after her, not believing that she had done that. He shook his head. He did need to speak with her. Obviously that was not happening at the moment.

Anna stared down at the papers, not having read them. She didn't feel any danger or fear from them. Sitting at her desk, her head bowed as she prayed over what she was about to read. The ringing of the doorbell disturbed her and had her on her feet, standing in front of the door and scowling at the man standing there. Jeremiah just had to show up, didn't he?

"Jeremiah? Should you even be here?" Anna stepped back as he moved into her space.

"I need to be. Anna? What have you gone and done?" Jeremiah studied the lady whom he had acknowledged in the wee early hours of the morning that he still loved deeply. He could only pray that she felt the same. If she didn't, then he had to release her. And that was something Jeremiah was struggling with. He didn't want to do that.

"Jeremiah? What am I do to with you? You're not safe to be out and about." Anna moved past him to study the street. "Where are your bodyguards?"

"I sent them home, Anna. They need that. They have been with me for far too long." Jeremiah reached to hug Anna, finding her resisting him at first before she hugged him back. "You're disturbed. What did you get?"

"A box of papers. Joe was here and wanted them. I refused. I don't feel any threat coming from them." Anna stared at the clock. "You might as well stay. I'll fix us something to eat and then you can go over the papers with me."

Jeremiah nodded, knowing that she was conceding to him being present when she read them and not that she really wanted him to be.

"How is your family, Anna?" Jeremiah stood awkwardly in the kitchen doorway, studying the soft peach of the walls, the off-white cabinets, and the wood-grained countertop. He looked down at the dark laminate flooring, liking what he saw.

"They're all fine. So far. I don't know if that will stay." Anna turned to look at him before she reached for a tray, finding Jeremiah's hands there first. "This way. I'm set up in my office."

"An office? Do you work from home, Anna?" Jeremiah was not familiar with the idea of each home having an office.

"No, I don't. I have an office, just like so many others." Her words were curt. She sighed. "I'm sorry, Jeremiah. I know that you don't understand homes nowadays. Most have a home office. Some people do work from home. I have one just because I had space for it. I use it for my volunteer work and for whatever else I need to do."

Jeremiah nodded, still not clear on the concept. He followed her and set the tray down on the coffee table in front of a comfortable love seat. He stood back to study the room, seeing the full book shelves that lined one wall, the bay window in another, and the French doors to the back yard.

"I like this, Anna. This is just the way I would have pictured your home. I dreamt so many times of what your home might look like." He turned, sadness on his face. "I missed you. I regret the years that we lost. I don't know where we go from here."

"I don't either, Jeremiah. We need to get to know one another again. We are not the same people that we were or that we would have been had we married. God has led us along this path for His purposes and plans. I have rebelled at times and had to seek His forgiveness." Anna sat, not watching

---

Jeremiah and not seeing the surprise and then acceptance at her words that crossed his face.

Chapter 18

Jeremiah reached for the papers as Anna returned to her seat. She had cleared away their meal and returned with a tray holding a pot of tea, two mugs, and whatever it was that they wanted in their tea. She sat, her head bowing for a moment. She just knew that when she read the papers, it would changer her life and likely Jeremiah's as well.

Reaching for Anna's hand, Jeremiah prayed for her and the situation that they found themselves in. He didn't know what to say other than beg God for His protection and help.

"Are you ready to read these?" Jeremiah pointed at the papers.

"I think so. I'm not sure what to think, Jeremiah. Do you?" Anna reached to take the papers from him, her eyes focusing on the top page. "What is this?"

Jeremiah leaned over to read the paper.

"It's a summary of what was found." He studied the name. "I'm not familiar with this person. Are you?"

Anna sighed. Of course, Abe would have been around. He must have left it after she retired.

"I do. Emma has a company where she finds people and brings them to justice. Her husband has a security team that trains other security teams. They have been involved with the girls. And now me." Anna blinked for a moment, understanding the deep friendship from this couple. "Emma always gives a concise summary of what she has found. And she releases nothing unless it has been verified and she has the proof to back up what she is saying." Anna grew quiet as she read through the papers, knowing that Jeremiah was reading them with her. It was something that they had done in the past, reading together. She just thought that habit had died with his disappearance.

Jeremiah sat back at last, troubled by what he had read and not sure why. He didn't know the people's names but he could tell that Anna did.

"Talk to me, Anna. Tell me what you are thinking."

"What I am thinking? That these people want to help us. They're not a danger to us. Emma has stated that. If she has researched and investigated them and come to that conclusion, then she is correct." Anna sat back into the corner of the love seat, her eyes on Jeremiah. "Some of them are new to town. Others have been here for generations. I don't know if you remember them or not. They are an older generation than us." She sighed. "I just pray that they are not in danger."

"He's not wanting to go after them. He wants us." Jeremiah had to tamp down his anger. He knew that he would have to deal with it later. "And I want to know why. It can't just be because I escaped his plans."

"No, it's not." Anna reached for the papers again, turning to the first page summary. "Emma states that. He's after us for more than that. If you had

---

not returned home, he would have just let you die overseas and left me grieving you. However, because you did come home, we are both in danger from him. His code seems to be to leave the families and friends alone, just to go after the people whom he thinks wronged him. And that would be us. You came home because this is your hometown and because of me. I'm targeted because of that too."

"That's true, Anna. It's so true. Now, how do we best him at his game?" Jeremiah grinned at her.

Anna drew in her breath. His grin was just like it had been years ago. She saw the younger Jeremiah for a moment, not the one with the lines in his face from what he had gone through.

"You're on, Jeremiah." Anna reached for her phone, seeing that Jeremiah had pulled out one too. "You need to get used to that." Anna gently took his phone, programming in every number that she could think of. "I've given you my number, the families' numbers, Joe's number, our friends' numbers. And we have many friends from here and surrounding towns that will help." She paused, a thought crossing her mind. "I don't understand, Jeremiah. How did he choose you?"

"We don't know, Anna. We've wracked our brains trying to determine that. All we can think of is that he is familiar with our town and for some reason decided that I needed to pay for something. We just don't know what." Jeremiah paused once more, uncertain as to how to continue. He no longer knew his town or its people.

<hr>

"That's okay, Jeremiah. It was a reach for you to even try to understand the undercurrents here in town." Anna sighed as her phone chimed. She glanced at the text message and then responded to Joe's question. No, the papers were not threatening. They came from Emma and if she wanted Joe to know anything of what she had sent, then Emma would send it to him. Joe just replied for Anna to stay safe.

Jeremiah rose at last, walking away from Anna's home. She stood on the front sidewalk, watching him, suddenly afraid for him. He had refused her offer to drive him home, simply shaking his head, hugging her, and turning away. Jeremiah didn't want to put her at risk. Instead, he would put himself at risk.

Ardan watched as the man walked away from his sister, turning on his car seat to study him. A memory niggled at his mind before he nodded. That was Jeremiah, wasn't it? He was out of the car and approaching his sister, his head ducked to study her face.

"Anna? Was that Jeremiah?" He hugged Anna before she shoved at him.

"It was. Come on in, Ardan. You need to read the paperwork from Emma. Maybe you'll find something that I'm missing or rather that Jeremiah and I are missing. He doesn't know his town any more."

"No, he doesn't." Ardan stepped back to where he could see the other man disappearing in the distance. "He shouldn't be out there walking on his own."

—

"I know. I offered him a ride but he refused. He's trying to take back the life that was stolen from him." Anna sank into her desk chair, watching as Ardan reached for the papers. "Read through them. Then talk to me." Anna turned to her computer, pulling up her email program and responding to what she needed to. She kept an eye on Ardan as she did so.

"Emma's concise summary is just that. I don't understand, even after what the boys went through, how she finds this information."

"And she can't explain it." Anna studied her brother, seeing the lines that had been etched into his face over the past couple of years. "Ardan, you and Bessie need a holiday."

"Not while this is going on, Anna. That's a given as the boys would say. We need to be where we can help you." Ardan studied his sister in turn.

"Right now? I don't see any danger. I may be naive but that is how life is." Anna sat back further in her chair. "Ardan? Who in town would do this to Jeremiah? Who hates him that much?"

Ardan nodded, his sister's thoughts echoing his.

"I think that there is someone. I wish I knew who. I would go after him if I could. And so would the boys and also you." Ardan prayed for his sister, begging God to protect her. "What can we do for you, Anna?"

"Do for me? Pray, I guess. And work to help solve this. Joe was around this morning but we didn't talk. I sent him away. I don't have any information

—

that would help him and he knows that. He was very curious about the box.”

“He was concerned for you, Anna, and rightly so.” Ardan soon rose, hugged his sister, and walked away. He knew that they would be speaking about this over and over. He just didn’t understand why or who.

Chapter 19

Jeremiah walked through the downtown area of his hometown, not greeting anyone or stopping. He was pacing out of frustration and worry, that much he knew. Anna had not responded to his phone call that morning and that worried him. It was Sunday and he should be in church. Only he didn't want to be there. He knew that if he did, people would question him as to where he had been for so many years. Jeremiah didn't know how to answer those questions without compromising the investigation. And that he absolutely refused to do.

Turning as he heard his name called, Jeremiah frowned at the man walking towards him. He didn't know him, he didn't think.

"Jeremiah? You don't remember me?" The young man grinned at him. "I'm Arlyn, Anna's nephew. It's been far too many years."

"It has been, Arlyn. I would not have recognized you." Jeremiah studied the younger man. "Why are you not in church?"

"I was hoping to find you. God understands when we're not there." Arlyn pointed towards a diner nearby. "Do you have time for a coffee or tea?" He waited patiently for Jeremiah to assess whether he did have the time to do just that.

"I do, Arlyn. I would like to catch up with you." Jeremiah slid onto a booth seat, his hand reaching for the menu. He studied it, not sure if he wanted anything or if he could afford anything to eat. His funds were limited at the moment until he started working again for David. And that would not be for a couple of weeks. He looked up as Arlyn cleared his throat.

"It's okay, Jeremiah. It's my treat. I understand that you haven't been working. Order what you want." Arlyn waved for the server and ordered them coffees to start with.

"Thank you then, Arlyn. Tell me about what you have been up to. I need to catch up with you three." Jeremiah gave a small smile, not sure if he should even be around the boys as he still termed them.

Arlyn did that, bringing more open smiles to Jeremiah's face as he described just what the triplets had been up to, their occupations, and more importantly, their wives and families. He could see the sadness on the older man's face.

"You didn't have a choice, Jeremiah. You were not here and not by your choice." Arlyn bit at his lip. "May I ask you a question?" At Jeremiah's nod, Arlyn still hesitated to speak. "When you left, how close were you and Aunt Anna?"

Jeremiah stared at him for a moment before he looked out of the window. He should have expected that question, given how close the boys were to their aunt.

"That's a fair question. I would have thought that you would have asked your aunt."

"We have, over the years. We asked if she had someone she loved and wanted to marry. She would just give a sad smile, hug us, and walk away without answering. We've talked between ourselves. We worry about her but would like to see her happy. So, how close were you two?" Arlyn waited patiently for the older man to speak. He knew that he was prying into something that he shouldn't. He could only pray for Jeremiah and Anna. Arlyn knew that whatever they were facing, either alone or as a couple, was far from over.

"That's a fair question, Arlyn. You know that your aunt and I were dating when you were young. We had become engaged two days before I left for overseas. We were going to host a dinner and let everyone know. You know what happened next."

Arlyn was sober and saddened as he listened to Jeremiah. He could not understand how God had allowed that to happen but he knew also that God had plans and purposes that no one could understand. He was also somewhat aware that Jeremiah and Anna were in danger now but there was nothing that he could go to and prove it.

"I know that you are in danger, Jeremiah. How does that affect Aunt Anna?" Arlyn was ready to take on the older man to protect a well-loved aunt.

"I am in danger, Arlyn. There is nothing that I can do to avoid it. If I had never come home, people here would just have forgotten me. However, there is someone here in town who means me harm. What that means for Anna? We're not sure. I know that she has spoken with Joe and someone named Emma has sent her information."

Arlyn gave a quick grin. It was good that Emma had gotten involved.

"Emma's in on this? That's good. She's a good friend of ours and works to find what she can to help. Her husband has a security team and will move in if he needs to." Arlyn grinned for a moment. "And we have two other friends on security teams. There are other friends who will become involved. I can guarantee you that."

"There are?" Jeremiah sighed before he reached for his mug of coffee and sipped at it. He then cradled it in his hands. "Times have changed so much, Arlyn. I'm trying to get up to speed on life today but it's hard. The conditions that I existed in were very primitive. The only lifeline I had was God. He was there with me all the time. Sure, I did suffer the first few months with beatings and deprivation but he worked in the men who were our guards. I was allowed a Bible after a year or two. That is what I had to cling to. Now? I have no idea how to live."

"We understand that, Jeremiah, as much as we can. We'll work with you gladly to help." Arlyn looked up as he felt someone near him and slid over to let Joe sit with him. "Joe? Are you not working today?"

"I was. But I saw you and Jeremiah and wondered if I could join you two just as a friend?" Joe grinned at Jeremiah.

"Joe? As a friend? I thought that you were the investigator." Jeremiah was puzzled at Joe's words.

"I am, Jeremiah. But I set aside the investigation to be there for my friends. It's hard to do and I have to remind myself not to take notes or remember anything said while I am in friend mode. God helps me to do that." Joe looked up with thanks as a plate of food was set in front of him. He asked a quick blessing before he eyed Jeremiah again. "Not in church today?"

"No, I didn't want to be. I feel too dangerous to be there. Besides, there would be too many questions asked if I did go there. People who knew me in the past would want to know what happened."

Joe nodded, turning slightly to look at Arlyn.

"Arlyn? You had a thought?"

"I did. Can we do a news article or special interest piece or have the police public relations department put out information on Jeremiah? Tell what we can of his story? Maybe that would bring out the one or ones responsible."

"That's an interesting question, Arlyn." Joe had thought of that but had not taken it any further. "Let me run it by my supervisor and see what he says."

"He doesn't need to approve it if Jeremiah decides to go ahead and speak with the press. We want you on our side but we understand." Arlyn shared a look with Jeremiah, seeing the understanding on his face.

"Don't do it, Arlyn." Joe stared down at his meal before he was on his feet, walking away. He had to be on another crime scene but he was very afraid that

Jeremiah would talk that step and put himself and Anna in even more danger.

Chapter 20

Joe ran for Anna's home late that afternoon, dodging the raindrops that had begun to fall. She had called him, panic in her voice, which was totally not her, he knew. He pounded at the front door before he reached for the knob, surprised that it turned under his hand. Joe reached for his weapon, gripping it in both hands as he wiped his feet on the mat inside the door and then began a systemic search of the house. He stopped in the office door way, surprise on his face as he watched Anna glaring at him, anger in her eyes.

Reaching for the gag and then untying her, Joe frowned at her before his hand was up to stop her words. He needed patrol officers and the crime scene team there and requested those very people. His hand was on Anna's arm, drawing her to her feet and then outside to a seat in his car.

"Anna? What happened?" Joe's gaze was searching the area, seeing some of her neighbours watching the increasing activity in the quiet, serene neighbourhood.

"What happened? How dare you ask me that? What do you think happened? I didn't tie myself up or gag myself just for the fun of it." Anna's angry words drew a smile to Joe's face. "And stop smiling. It's not funny."

"No, it's not. But this is not how I have ever seen you react." Joe nodded at the patrol officer who was pointing towards the back yard.

"No, you have not but then you have never seen me bound and gagged before. The two men were wearing masks and tried to disguise their voices. They were Ed and Fred Spencer."

"They were? We also suspected something about them, didn't we?" Joe was not surprised that she named them. He was surprised that they had shown up at Anna's house. "How are they involved in this?"

"They were muttering about Jeremiah and how he had to pay. What did they mean?" Anna was out of Joe's car and running towards where the police tape was strung. Ducking under it, she just hugged Jeremiah who had appeared to speak with her. That wasn't happening, not at that point.

Joe shook his head at her actions. She shouldn't have done that but then again, they were engaged, weren't they? He just didn't know if they would stay that way. God had them in the hollow of His hand and was protecting them.

Jeremiah looked past Anna towards her house. He wasn't sure what had happened but something had happened to his lady.

"Anna? What happened?"

"Someone broke into my house and tied me up. Joe showed up for some reason." Anna stalked back towards Joe, intent on finding out why he had appeared. This action was just out of character for her that it surprised Joe. "Joe? What happened? I know that I managed to call you but I don't understand why those men were there. Do you?"

"Not at the moment, Anna. We have to look into everything." Joe sighed. "And you need a security system."

"Absolutely not. I won't have that." Anna walked away again, heading this time for Ardan.

"Anna?" Ardan simply hugged his sister before he turned her back to watch her house, keeping an arm around her.

"We need to talk, Ardan, and with the rest of the family. Someone tied me up and gagged me. Ed and Fred Spencer. They were muttering something about Jeremiah. They're too young to know him."

"They are. We'll figure it out. Send the names off to Emma and she'll discover what they have been up to and who employs them." Ardan's arm tightened around her shoulders. "I'm afraid for you, Anna."

"Don't do God's work for Him, Ardan. He's protecting us even though it doesn't appear that He is."

"I know that He is. I just don't want to see you in danger just as the boys were." Ardan studied his sister's face, seeing emotions flittering across it. "Anna?"

"It's too late for that, Ardan. I have discovered that I have been watched since before Jeremiah disappeared. They have kept in the shadows. Now that Jeremiah is free and back in his hometown? They are coming out and coming after me. That's what we think happened today." Anna was not happy that she had been threatened that day and without knowing exactly who had been behind that situation.

Ardan stared down at her and then his focus went to the man standing next to Anna. Jeremiah had appeared, despite the protest of Carl and his team. Jeremiah had simply told them that they were no longer protecting him, despite having done that for months. They just needed to let him live his life. Carl had stepped back at the words sent his way and nodded. Jeremiah was taking back his life, no matter what anyone else said.

"Jeremiah?"

Ardan's soft voice caught Anna's attention. Anna shifted in how she was standing to glance up at the tall man standing beside her. She could see anger on his face and sighed. He didn't need to be here but he was. He was trying to look after her once more. Anna wasn't sure how she felt about that now, given that she no longer knew the man standing beside her.

"Jeremiah? What are you doing here?" Anna's words brought his attention to her.

"Looking for you. What happened?" Jeremiah just reached for her hand, not feeling her trying to withdraw hers.

"I was tied up in my office. That's what happened." Anna sighed, begging God to forgive her anger. "I named the two men to Joe. You wouldn't know them."

"Who were they?" Jeremiah waited patiently for Anna to speak. He had learned that about her in the short time that he had been around her once more. She needed to think through her words. This was a shift in her that he had to acknowledge was likely related to his disappearance.

"Ed and Fred Spencer." Anna's voice was quiet. She felt the tightened grip on her hand. "Jeremiah?"

"Spencer? As in Edward senior?" At her nod, Jeremiah sighed. "He was around where I was kept captive. He's involved in some way." His eyes met those of Joe who had approached him. "Joe?"

"Do you know the father?" Joe drew Jeremiah to one side, sighing as Jeremiah dragged Anna with him.

"I do. He's been known to walk the edge of crime when we were teenagers and young adults. Of course, I don't know if he is still involved or even still alive. I have not had contact with him as you well know, other than for him showing up in that country." Jeremiah dropped Anna's hand to wrap an arm around her, surprising her.

Joe stared at him in surprise before his eyes closed. He now needed to track down the father and that would be difficult as he seemed to have disappeared from town.

Joe dropped down into his desk chair, his hand out to ruffle through all the file folders sitting on his desk. He was exhausted, he decided, and needed that vacation that he kept putting off. He just didn't see how he could go away. Joe looked up as his supervisor approached his office and then entered, closing the door behind him.

"Joe? You need to take that vacation." David watched him for a moment. "And that is not a suggestion. Let me know where you stand on your cases and then I want you to leave for at least a week."

Joe nodded knowing that David was correct. He did need to leave but he didn't want to abandon anyone, and that included Anna and Jeremiah.

"I will. Here's what is on my desk." Joe always had a concise summary of each case, updating it as he found new information. "The one that I am most concerned about? That's Jeremiah and Anna. I don't get a sense of who it is that is behind him."

"I hear that you arrested the Spencer boys today. Is their father involved?" David watched Joe's reaction closely.

"Jeremiah said that he did show up where he was imprisoned. Spencer senior is keeping a very low profile here in town."

"He always has. We have had rumours about him since before you were born but no one has been able to prove anything." David was frustrated at that.

His thought was that if it had been proven years ago, then maybe Jeremiah and Anna would not have been separated.

Joe walked away from his office shortly after that, a sense of freedom and relief washing through him. He needed this break and knew exactly where he was heading. He didn't see the car following him as he drove away. Two hours later, Joe pulled into a small campground, heading for a reserved cabin. He was friends with the owners and knew that he would be able to unwind there. Joe just didn't see the car that followed him in and then drove directly at him as he walked to the cabin. Hearing a sound, Joe jumped to the side of the road, just not quite making it in time. His body rolled across the lawn of the cabin as onlookers ran towards him and others tried to follow the car. They just weren't successful.

David looked up an hour later as a patrol officer appeared in his doorway. On his feet, David ran for his vehicle and then for the hospital. Joe was still unconscious and David could only pray for his friend and fellow investigator. This was not what was needed at this point.

Anna stepped back from her front door that evening, watching as David entered. She frowned at him and studied the stressed look on his face.

"David? You're here?" Anna pointed towards the living room, finding her favourite chair and watching as David sank down on the couch. Something was wrong, she knew, and waited somewhat impatiently for him to speak.

"Anna? We have to bring in a new investigator on Jeremiah's case. I sent Joe off on his vacation that he desperately needed. He was run down in the campground just as he arrived. He's alive and conscious but he's battered to some extent. We need to let him heal."

Anna drew in a deep breath, a hand over her mouth. She had expected something like this but had prayed that Joe would stay safe.

"His family?"

"They're out of town and out of reach. I'm not sure exactly where they are. Would one of the boys know?" David was grasping at straws, he knew.

"They might. Let me send them a text." Anna looked up at a sound from David. "David?"

"It's better if it comes from me in an official capacity." David studied his friend. They had been in college together and David and his wife, Eve, had not walked away from Anna as some of their friends had when Jeremiah disappeared. They did not blame her for that. None of them had understood it at the time.

"Okay. This is odd, David. He's off duty, correct?" At his nod, Anna sighed. "They take him out and it has to start all over. That allows more time for someone to get to Jeremiah and take him out as the boys would say."

"Those are my thoughts. As to the investigator, I'm not sure which one to assign. They have history here in town that precludes them from taking on some of his cases, including the one involving you."

"Then, you'll be the one, won't you?" Anna was nodding. "Let us pray for you, David. You'll be bearing a bigger and harder load until Joe is back. I would presume that he will be off for a while."

"For at least this week, perhaps longer. We don't know as yet." David prayed with his friend and then walked away, not satisfied that he had accomplished anything other than worrying her. His next stop was Jeremiah.

Jeremiah stared at David for a moment. He remembered David from years past and knew that he had stayed a true friend to Anna.

"You're saying that you have to start over with my case?" Jeremiah could hear the frustration that David was not voicing. "I don't know, David. It sounds as if Joe was getting close to something that might break the case open."

"That's what I thought. I will be sitting down with you tomorrow, Jeremiah, if I may, just to go over what happened and where the investigation stands." David prayed with his old friend, disturbed that Jeremiah had been lost to their friends' group for so long.

"I will look forward to that. Anna's nephews have mentioned friends that are now involved." Jeremiah wasn't sure that he had heard them correctly or how those said friends would help.

David grinned. Emma had been in touch, sensing that something had happened. She was sending him more information than he knew what to do with at the moment, but he knew that she was always spot on with her work.

Jeremiah stood with his hand braced on the door frame as he watched David walk back to his car. This had not been the news that he wanted to hear but to tell the truth, he had fully expected it. He was just thankful that God had protected Joe.

Chapter 22

Joe walked slowly towards Anna's home two days later. He was not to be working but he could not help himself. Anna watched her young friend before she sighed. He just had to do that, didn't he, Lord? He needs the healing that only You can give and to find the rest that he desperately needs.

"Joe? You shouldn't be here." Anna reached to tuck a hand around his arm.

"I know, Anna. I can't stay away. I know that David is investigating. But I still need to know what you are thinking." Joe turned slightly as he heard footsteps. "And Jeremiah is here."

"He is. He's not supposed to be out in the open." Anna scowled at Jeremiah, finding him just grinning at her before he followed the two into her house and locked the door behind him.

Jeremiah could not help himself. He had to show up at Anna's. Not only was he worried about her, but he really wanted to renew their friendship and see where it went. He sighed to himself. That friendship was in God's hands and only He could determine what their path would be. He prayed for God's protection on them and also healing for Joe.

"Joe? How are you?" Jeremiah watched their young friend closely.

Joe shrugged. He had no way of knowing how he should feel. He was battered and bruised but God had protected him. The car had missed him as he threw himself away from it but the ground had been hard and he had fallen forcefully onto it.

"I'm getting there. This was not how I was planning on spending my vacation." His hand went up as the two with him protested. "God protected me. He also knew that this would happen. I can only give praise for His hand on me." He looked between the two. "What has happened?"

"What has happened?" Anna frowned for a moment. "Nothing has, Joe. That surprises me. I feel watched when I am out and about and when I am at work. No one in the family have said anything this week about being followed or watched."

"It's the same for me, Joe. God is here. He has walked this path before us and knows exactly what we are facing. We have to trust in Him." Jeremiah studied the younger man. "How close are you to finding Spencer senior?"

Joe shook his head. Jeremiah just had to ask that question, didn't he?"

"We haven't found him. A friend is searching for him but says that he has gone undercover somewhere in town." Joe was frustrated at that as well. "Where would you look for him?"

"Where would I look? I don't know the town any more, Joe. I have no idea where he would have been hanging out even all those years ago. Anna?" Jeremiah turned to watch her.

Anna raised her head, nodding. Joe was asking the questions that she expected him to ask at this point.

"He has a number of hiding spaces and places, Joe. That's been rumoured over time. They are spread out across the city and in the downtown area and also in the affluent areas." Anna was on her feet, heading for her office and returning with a file folder. "Here. These are ones that I know about or that someone has told me about. I have not given it to David as yet but have passed it on to Emma. She has someone looking into them." Anna sighed. "I want this over, Joe, and now."

Joe grinned at her for a moment before he turned to Jeremiah.

"Jeremiah? What can we do for you?"

Jeremiah shrugged. He had no idea what anyone could do for him. He didn't feel as if he had friends in town any more but he knew that was just his emotions playing with him. He had been approached by old friends and new friends. Jeremiah was just too cautious to have much contact with them.

"I don't know, Joe, other than to keep Anna safe and to solve this. I don't know the people in this town any more. My friends? They are approaching me but I am hesitant to get involved in any friends' activities. I just feel too unsafe."

"It's normal to feel that way, Jeremiah, even if you had lived here in town all your life. With what you went through? You're not sure who you can trust and who would mean you harm. You feel safe with Anna and her family, just because you know her that well. Whether or not you continue as a couple? That is up to you and to God. I see you married but it's not what

I want. It's what is in God's will for you both." Joe rose, grimacing slightly with pain. He always felt better when he heard Anna's prayers for him. "Thank you, Anna. Your prayers are always so welcome." He walked away, Anna following him to shut the door and lock it.

She hesitated to move back to the living room, hearing Jeremiah's footsteps as he headed for the kitchen. Her head went back for a moment as she looked up at the ceiling. Jeremiah was making himself at home and she wasn't sure what she thought about that. Anna turned to stare out of the door window, watching the vehicle that slowed and then parked in front of her house. It wasn't someone from the neighbourhood. She reached for her phone, snapping a picture of the vehicle, and then sending it on to David. Anna would not forward it to Joe just yet. She would let David take care of that.

Jeremiah turned as he felt a hand on his arm and then simply hugged Anna. That took her by surprise. He stepped back from her, his eyes shadowed for a moment.

"Anna, how do we do this? How do we solve this?"

"We meet with my family. That's planned for tomorrow. Now, you are invited. It's up to you whether you come or not. And friends who are actively working this case will be there. They are from out of town." Anna took her mug of tea with thanks and then pointed to the back door. "I need to be outside, Jeremiah."

"We can do that." Jeremiah followed her, not sure what had just happened. Was he being included in her family once more? This had to be God at work, he knew. Anna had been reluctant to allow him contact with the boys and their families. This was changing, he could see. "Thank you, Anna. Your invitation is welcome. I would like to meet with your family. Arlyn did track me down a few days ago just to talk."

"He did. He had asked me if he should. I just let him make his own decision. That's only fair." Anna's eyes closed for a moment as the swing rocked gently. "You need to get to know them, Jeremiah. They often asked about you when this first happened. Once in a while, they would ask if I had heard from you. I could only say no. Now that you're back, this has changed."

"It has. God will protect them, Anna. We'll see to that." He reached for her hand, not finding that she was preventing him from taking it. "I missed you so much, Anna. Your presence in my life is part of what kept me going over the years. I don't know where we stand yet, but God has not told me to stay away from you." Jeremiah was on his feet, walking around the house and finding his car.

Anna had risen to her feet, a hand covering her mouth as she choked back sobs. He was still trying to protect and love her. She just didn't know where her own emotions stood.

Chapter 23

Ardan watched his family closely the next day. The triplets and their families had arrived as had a number of their friends. He shook his head. He was glad that he had a roomy house but this was pushing the limits. Anna stood beside him, Jeremiah beside her. He had arrived at her house and asked that she ride with him. He didn't know where Ardan lived any more, he simply stated with a grin. Anna had shaken her head at him and then walked to his car, waiting for him to unlock it.

Bessie stood where she could watch both Anna and Ardan. She knew that her husband was deeply troubled about Anna but they could only do so much, they both knew. Her attention then went to Jeremiah. Bessie could see the changes in him from his time overseas and that disturbed her. By all rights, Anna and Jeremiah should have married and raised their own family. That was taken from them. She sighed. God was in control of this, she knew, and had to repent of her anger and also her distrust of Jeremiah. Bessie was not completely convinced that he had been held a prisoner all those years despite what the evidence showed. Evidence could be faked, she knew.

Cayce moved in on his mother, an arm around her shoulders.

"Aunt Anna and Jeremiah came together? I didn't think that they would."

"They did. Apparently, he showed up at her home and insisted that she come with him." Bessie swung an arm around her youngest son. "Everyone is here?"

"They are. Abe and Emma were the last to arrive." Cayce looked around. "We're spending time in prayer first?"

"We are, son." Ardan had moved that way. "We need to. Then, we start looking at what we have. I don't know if this is such a good idea, with another country involved, but we will work it just as we did for you three. I just didn't expect another of our family to face danger like this."

"None of us did, Dad." Cayce moved away, finding Haley and their twins before he settled on the floor in the living room, Haley curled up tight to him.

Ardan nodded at Abe who simply bowed his head and prayed. The others followed before Abe raised his head to study each of the ones gathered. As a security expert, he knew the danger that was growing towards the couple and wanted to prevent their deaths. His wife, Emma, was on her feet, passing out the information that she had gathered. She could not tell anyone how she found the information. It was just how her mind and her computer programs worked.

Emma hesitated as she neared Anna, a thought running through her mind. She found her laptop and began a new search, knowing that she had to. She turned to the group once more, her eyes on Anna before it moved to Jeremiah.

"Anna? What can you tell me about what you are going through?" Emma waited patiently for Anna to speak, seeing her sharing a look with Jeremiah.

———

"I'm not sure what to say, Emma. How do I describe my thoughts and feelings?" Anna looked at the younger woman. "I'm also not sure how I feel about Jeremiah any more."

"That's understandable, Anna. It's been that many years and you no longer know one another enough to continue with what your plans were." Emma sighed. "How can I help?"

Anna shrugged. She had no words to properly express how she felt. Her eyes were on Jeremiah as he sat across the room from her, Joe and Briar flanking him.

"I don't want to hurt him any more than he has been hurt, but I am afraid that I will without meaning to. I mean, we are talking but with what he's gone through and it not being over, he's afraid for anyone that he gets close to." Anna looked up to see Jeremiah watching her even as he conversed with her nephews.

"He's hurting, Anna. He doesn't know where he belongs any more. He doesn't recognize his town or the people here. Society has changed so much, particularly over the last few years. He has to reacclimatize himself once more. We have difficulty at times with society and the changes in technology that are here. I can't imagine how it is for him." Emma bit at her lip for a moment. "I can have Micah stop by and help him to understand today's technology. Any one of our guys would do that. You know that. You also know others who would help."

"We do." Anna looked up as she felt an arm around her. Jeremiah had moved to sit beside her, a questioning look on his face. "Jeremiah?"

"It's okay, Anna. I know that I am very much out of touch with life and society today." Jeremiah had a sad look on his face. "I'm trying to catch up." He nodded at the triplets. "They have volunteered to help as has Joe." He drew in a deep breath. "I just worry about you. I don't want to see you hurt and I am afraid that is exactly what will happen."

"I know, Jeremiah. You are in danger as well." Anna shared a look with Emma who was watching Jeremiah carefully with deep concentration. "How do you stay safe?"

Jeremiah shrugged. He had no idea how to do that. He didn't know the safe spots in town any more, not as he had when he was a younger man. Jeremiah worried about Anna as well. He had been told by Carl and Greg that she was being watched and followed, and their thinking was that this was being done to get to him.

Walking through her house late that evening, Anna prayed for her family and then for Jeremiah. She had no idea how to feel about him, not any more. She had conflicting emotions about him and was praying through those feelings. Anna didn't have a sense that God wanted her to walk away from the man who she had loved all those years ago and yes, she had to admit to herself, still loved. Anna just didn't know where they were heading.

Pausing at the front window, Anna parted the drapes enough to peek outside. The car was still parked in front of her home and she could see the red spark from a lit cigarette. She sighed. This was not what she wanted. She couldn't get a real good look at the car but she knew that it had been there for hours. Whoever it was? They were keeping watch on her and that she didn't like.

Anna finally retired, tears on her cheeks as she slept. Her sleep was restless and nightmare filled, she knew when she awoke in the morning. She just couldn't remember those dreams and really didn't want to. Rising, she headed for her prayer corner, her Bible in her hand as she sought to find comfort and peace in the situation. She knew that God was with her and protecting her. She just didn't feel that comfort and peace. Anna sighed once more and rose, heading into her day, not knowing what that day would bring.

Chapter 24

Walking through his neighbourhood the next day, Jeremiah was lost in thought and not really focusing on his surroundings. He was troubled by what had been discussed the day before. Abe had sought him out and drew him to one side, going over what they knew. Jeremiah had nodded. He knew just how vicious the man was who had imprisoned him, even better than the man who had sat beside him and described what they had discovered about him. To say that Abe was worried was an understatement.

Turning as he heard footsteps, Jeremiah frowned at the man approaching him. No, he decided, he didn't know him. He stood, watching as the man approached him, not saying anything as the man stopped in front of him.

The younger man simply watched Jeremiah, his eyes catching sight of the two men who had approached Jeremiah from behind. They had the older man where they wanted him. Jeremiah would disappear and never appear again.

"You're coming with us." The man's voice was harsh and rough.

Jeremiah just stared at him even as he felt the prick of a knife through his sweatshirt. He had tasted freedom once more and there was no way that he was leaving his hometown or even leaving to go anywhere with these men. God was with him, he knew, and would only allow what was in His plans for Jeremiah.

"No, I don't think so." Jeremiah just stood still, not moving, not wanting to be harmed in any way.

"Oh, but you see, you are." The man in front of him nodded at the men behind him. "I have friends here who will make sure that you do."

Jeremiah shook his head. He saw Joe walking towards him and heard footsteps behind him. He moved slightly, knowing that help was at hand. He just didn't expect the knife to be driven into him, crumbling him to the sidewalk. His vision darkened even as he heard shouts from above him.

Joe ran forward, tackling the first man and taking him down. He struggled to clap the handcuffs on him as a patrol officer moved in to help him. He could hear the shouts from the other officers as they fought with the other two men to subdue them and take them into custody. On his feet, Joe stared down at Jeremiah as the paramedics who had been summoned worked over him. This was not what was to happen. Joe had received word from the street that Jeremiah was to disappear that day and he wanted to prevent that. He just had not been able to prevent Jeremiah from being hurt, and just how hurt he was, Joe didn't know.

Turning at a touch on his arm, Joe moved away to speak with David.

"What happened, Joe?" David was somewhat in shock.

"They had approached him. We weren't able to get to him in time before he was stabbed." Joe blew out a breath. "I need to stay here but I also need to get to Anna. She needs to be with him. For all intents and purposes, she is his next of kin. It doesn't matter how long it's been."

"I know. Head off and find her. We'll work this for you. We'll talk, Joe, and soon. For now, stay with Anna." David watched Joe walk away before he turned to the patrol officers who remained. He didn't have to tell them how to do what was needed to be done. They were all experienced officers, some of them friends with the Koyle family.

Anna stared at Joe in horror as she stood in her office at her workplace. She could see her employer standing behind Joe, waiting for her to move towards the exit. This was a dangerous time, Joe knew only too well. Anna could very well disappear and not be found. That was something they were working to prevent. Patrol officers surrounded the building, watching for anyone who didn't belong and were ready to pull out around Joe's vehicle to safely convey Anna to the hospital.

"There must be someone else who can go, Joe. It's not my right." Anna was protesting even as she reached for her purse and locked her office door.

"No, there isn't. You know that, Anna. Being engaged to him, no matter what has happened in the intervening years? That makes you his next of kin. Now, are you ready to come with us? If you don't, I'm prepared to make it a police directive." Joe was not backing down from Anna. She needed to be with Jeremiah and he needed her with him.

Anna's hand shook as she fastened the seatbelt and then stared out at the patrol vehicles around her.

Joe had been right, she decided. She could have disappeared and not been returned to her family. That scared her. All she could do at present was pray for God's protection and then prayed for Jeremiah, not knowing how badly that he was hurt.

Sitting in the waiting room of the Emergency Department, Anna's thoughts went back over how many times she had done that in the last few years. She was on her own for the moment, not seeing the officers who stood near her, on watch for anyone who would approach her that shouldn't.

Anna felt an arm around her and turned slightly. Ardan had been shocked as well when Joe had reached out to him and asked that he come and stay with Anna. She needed her family with her.

"Anna? Any word?" Ardan's voice was kept low, his heart praying for his beloved sister.

"Not yet. They're still assessing him, the clerk said. They'll come find me when they are ready for that." Anna shifted uncomfortably on her chair, not wanting to be there but knowing that Jeremiah really didn't have any family who could step in.

"I know that you don't. You're struggling to accept that fact that he is back in your life. You still love him, I know, Anna, but you're not sure about the last years and how that affects your relationship. You kept a lot hidden from us." Ardan's hand went up as Anna opened her mouth to protest. "You did it first to protect yourself and then to protect us. I know you that well, sis."

"That's so true, Ardan. I did it to protect my heart. I thought that he had left me for another woman and had forgotten about me. I never dreamed that he was kept away from me." She laid her head against her brother's shoulder. "This is hard, Ardan. I know that God has protected us and returned Jeremiah to our lives. He had a chance to grow in his relationship with God that he would never have had if he hadn't been imprisoned. We've talked about that. He acknowledges that God was there and that God's promises to never leave him and to protect and heal him were what he needed at the time. But now? I don't want to be out there as his loved one. I'm not sure if that will ever happen."

Ardan nodded. Anna was expressing what he and Bessie and yes, his sons and their wives, had discussed. He had often wondered if Anna had been engaged to Jeremiah and not said anything. That fact had turned out to be true. He had spoken with Anna whose silence just the week previous had confirmed his suspicions.

Chapter 25

Rising to her feet as Joe approached her, Anna's hand reached for Ardan's. Ardan had no intention of leaving his sister as she walked towards the examination rooms. Joe watched her closely, knowing that she really didn't want to be there but as a friend of Jeremiah's, she would not refuse. It is not in the character of any of the Koyles to walk away from a friend.

Anna paused in the doorway as her eyes found the bed. She drew in a deep breath before she walked carefully towards Jeremiah. Her hand covered her mouth for a moment before it found Jeremiah's arm. She didn't know what to say or even think at that point.

Turning as she heard footsteps, Anna faced the surgeon who had returned to speak with her.

"Anna? May I call you that?" At her nod, the surgeon went on to describe what Jeremiah's injuries were. "We need to do surgery, Anna. He has internal bleeding and we need to assess what other damage has been done." He frowned. "I understand that you are engaged to him?"

Anna sighed. This is not how she wanted this out there.

"I would ask that you keep that confident, Doctor. I don't want it out there. We were engaged many years ago before Jeremiah disappeared overseas. He was held captive for many years before he was freed and able to return home. At present? We engaged in name only, not sure where we are going as a couple. I don't want anyone and I repeat anyone to put it out there."

The surgeon frowned at her. This is not what he expected to hear. He turned as he heard a throat clearing.

Joe stood beside the surgeon, his eyes on Anna before they moved to the surgeon.

"It is extremely important, Doctor, that you do as she requests. Jeremiah is under police guard. And Anna is at risk as well. If any word gets out about their engagement from years ago, that person who did it will be arrested and charged. Make sure that doesn't happen." Joe was stern, knowing that he had to be.

The surgeon stared at Joe before he nodded. He knew only too well how privacy laws worked.

"We'll do our best to ensure that."

"Do more than your best, Doctor." Anna stared at him. "If anything gets out about myself or Jeremiah by anyone here on staff or as a visitor, you will be hearing from my lawyer." Anna refused to back down from him. "And I will see that charges are laid."

Joe was nodding.

"She's right. To speak about this is a huge liability to the hospital and anyone who speaks out of turn. It would be a clear violation of Jeremiah's privacy."

The surgeon stared at them before he nodded. He then turned to Jeremiah, re-assessing him.

"We need to take him to surgery. The wound needs to be addressed and we need to assess what internal damage has been done." He went on to explain to Anna just what they would be doing and then handed her the clipboard that held the surgical consents.

Anna read them over, troubled that she had to do this. She felt as if she was having to consent to surgery for a stranger. Joe's arm came around her shoulders and he prayed for her.

"Anna?" Ardan's arm came around his sister as Joe moved away. "He would do the same for you. Think about that. You're the only one who knows him well enough to know even a part of what he would want." He prayed for her, asking for peace and comfort for his sister and for healing for Jeremiah. He then shocked the surgeon by praying for him and the surgical team. The surgeon had never been present at such a prayer before.

Walking away from her brother, Anna paused in the hallway to turn back and study Jeremiah. She sighed. This is not where she wanted to be, not at all. She walked away, leaving Ardan to search for her.

Ardan paused, not finding his sister. That concerned him. She needed to be there, he thought, and began to search harder, not finding her at all. Any attempts to raise her on her phone were ignored.

Anna walked through her house and then stared into her closet. She sighed. She had lived in a house that Jeremiah and she had talked of. Her clothing were the colours that he had liked her in. That had to change she decided. Anna needed to take back her life.

Reaching for her phone, Anna made the call that would cause consternation in her family and certainly with Jeremiah. She listed her house for sale and then went with her real estate friend to look at a condominium. Papers were signed that day to purchase one. And her home also sold that day.

Friends moved in to help her pack and then to move. She didn't contact her family, knowing that they were away for a week on a family vacation. There would be time to face the music when they returned.

Anna turned two weeks later from the French doors that led to her balcony. She was content, she thought. She had no idea of the consternation and concern and yes, fear, that her sudden move caused. She was planning on a trip beginning tomorrow with a friend, a long overdue vacation.

Jeremiah walked slowly up to Anna's home ten days later. He had searched for Anna to come every day. She just didn't appear. He needed to see her. Jeremiah's steps were slow and cautious. He still felt unsteady on his feet, something that was concerning to the physicians treating him. Ringing the doorbell, he turned to study the area. It didn't look like Anna's home any more, he had just decided as the door opened.

The young man standing there and holding a toddler waited for Jeremiah to speak.

"I'm sorry. I was looking for Anna." Jeremiah frowned at the young man.

"No, Anna doesn't live here now. We moved in a week ago. It was a really quick sale." He gave a compassionate smile. "I don't know where she is."

Jeremiah walked slowly from the house, his feet dragging. He had no idea how to find her. He had tried to call her but her voice mail picked up quickly. He looked up, begging God to help him find her. He just needed to see her and to hear her voice.

Chapter 26

Anna turned as her friend, Maria, called to her. A huge smile lit her face. She was happy being at this rustic cottage on the shore of Lake Erie just fifteen minutes from town.

"I am so glad we did this, Anna. We both needed this, but you more than me."

"We did, Maria. I feel as if I am finally free of the past and ready to move on."

Maria studied her friend. She knew only too well how much Anna had suffered over the years. She had been the only one whom Anna had confided in.

"Yes, you did. Now what? Where do you go with Jeremiah?" Maria waited patiently for Anna to respond, prayers rising for her friend.

Anna shrugged, not too sure how to respond. "I don't know. I walked away from him when he needed me. I have moved without telling anyone. I have changed my appearance to reflect the new me. I have no idea what my family or Jeremiah will think." Anna grew sober. She had been avoiding any calls or text messages, simply stating that she needed some time to think things through.

"What about the ring?"

"I slipped it through his mail slot. I am sure that he has it by now. I don't know that we have a future. Too much time has passed and we have both changed. God alone knows if our paths continue separately or together. I needed this time to think and pray and get some perspective without my family chiming in or Jeremiah coming around." Anna's face grew more sober. "He has no one other than me. I just don't know if I can be that one."

Maria nodded. Anna had been honest with her. All she could do was pray for her friend. Anna walked away at that point, needing some quiet time by herself. Maria watched her go before she quietly followed her. There was a real sense of danger growing around Anna and Maria didn't know from where or from whom.

Maria's steps paused for a moment as she struggled to understand what she could do to help Anna. Walking forward once more, her head jerked up as she heard a scream and then silence.

"Anna? Anna, are you okay?" Maria's steps halted as she frantically searched for Anna. Moving forward towards the rocks, her hands covered her mouth and stopped her scream. Maria scrambled over the rocks to where Anna lay in a crumpled heap, not moving.

The sound of a loud diabolical laugh echoed through the air, stopping Maria in her tracks. she froze, her hand once more covering her mouth to still her scream of fear. She spun in a circle, not seeing the man who had uttered the scream. Fear was still wafting through her body as she dropped to her knees beside Anna, desperately seeking a pulse. Anna was still alive but Maria knew that she needed help that she herself could not provide.

Thirty minutes later, Maria watched from the sidelines as the paramedics and firefighters worked to stabilize Anna. Anna was transferred to a wire stretcher and carried carefully from the area. Maria followed, Joe pacing beside her. He could not understand what had happened and with Maria not seeing the fall, he was at a loss to understand what had happened to the lady he considered an aunt.

Joe pocketed his phone once more as he stood and watched Anna being assessed. He could see the grim looks on the faces of the medical staff and knew that it would be a while before they had any answers. He for one was shocked at how Anna had changed her appearance including cutting her hair to a shorter style that brought out her curls. Joe walked away with no answers to give the family. He stood for a moment and studied his friends. Explaining the unexplainable was never easy.

Ardan looked up at that moment and then rose to approach Joe. Jeremiah was at his side, desperate to have news on the lady whom he now acknowledged that he still loved deeply. He just didn't know what her feelings were towards him.

The physician simply pointed to where Anna lay on a stretcher. She was alive, battered and bruised, but alive by the grace of God. She would be hurting, he knew, and there was nothing that they could do to prevent that. Only God could heal her. That His protection had been there was evident in the fact that she was not hurt worse than she was.

Ardan paused by his sister with his hand resting on her cheek. He had to blink back his tears. There was about ten years in an age gap between them. She was his adored and deeply loved little sister whom he had tried to protect all of her life. Now, it seemed as if that was not possible and he had to step back and let God do the protecting.

Jeremiah paused in the doorway, wanting to go in but not wanting to intrude on Ardan and Anna. He turned and walked away, finding Joe waiting for him. Joe drew the older man away from the rooms and to the outside where he simply stood and prayed for his friend. The triplets had followed the two and surrounded them as they all prayed.

Ardan looked around as the physician approached and assessed Anna once more. His mouth opened to ask his questions before he snapped it closed.

"Ardan? That is you?" The physician waited patiently for Ardan to nod. "Your sister is very fortunate. I know you are a praying man. God protected her greatly. From what I have been told, she fell on some pretty rough rocks. Aside from bruising and a concussion, she is unharmed. It is as if she fell onto something cushiony."

"God did that. He protected her." Ardan blinked away his tears. "When can we take her home?"

"Soon. We'll let the IV run and then see how she is." The physician paused. "This was deliberate. Find the ones responsible. She may not survive another attack."

Ardan nodded as he heard footsteps approaching. Bessie's arm was around him as she and the three younger ladies appeared.

Simply shaking his head, Ardan was unable to speak. Instead, he hugged the three ladies before he walked away to find his sons and yes, the man who seemed determined not to walk away from Anna.

Chapter 27

Anna stared at her brother before she simply shook her head and walked away. She didn't need his hovering and that was exactly what he was doing. She had been discharged that morning and Ardan had insisted that she come to his home. Anna had not been prepared to do that but for the sake of peace had done so.

Ardan turned for a moment to answer a question from Bessie. When he turned back to find his sister, she was gone. He heard the soft closure of the front door and almost ran that way to find her. Wrenching open the door, he didn't see her despite his almost frantic running to the road. Anna had simply disappeared.

Jeremiah had approached the house as Anna had exited it. He had reached for her hand, finding hers clinging to his.

"Where do you want to go, Anna?" Jeremiah tugged her to his car and shoved her inside before he slid behind the wheel.

Anna shrugged. She really didn't know where she wanted to be other than away from her family. That was not her, she knew. She just felt such a sense of fear and terror when she was around them.

"I don't know, Jeremiah. I really don't know. Take me home, I guess." Anna didn't see the look that was shot her way before Jeremiah pulled away from the curb and drove off.

"Where is home, Anna?" Jeremiah studied the lady whom he loved deeply, seeing the changes that she had made in her appearance over the last couple of weeks. "You've changed your hair. I like all the curls."

Anna snorted, knowing full well why she had taken that step. She had kept herself the same for over twenty years, waiting for Jeremiah to return and grieving at the same time. She was taking back her life.

"I had to change, Jeremiah. I just had to."

"I know, sweetheart. I do know that. I have to as well." Jeremiah stopped at a local coffee shop, running in and returning with coffees and muffins for them both. "We need to talk, Anna." He watched as her composure crumbled to some extent and then reached to hug her.

"We do, Jeremiah. I needed some time." Anna looked up at her, her eyes tear drenched. "Where do we go from here? I know who is behind this. It's not who you think. Just before I was pushed off that rock, the name was said aloud and that he wanted me to die in retaliation for your escape."

Jeremiah was watching her closely, his heart breaking for his lady. He could see the love that she had for him shining in her eyes. He uttered a name, seeing the confirmation of it in her eyes.

"Marry me, sweetheart. We'll fight him together. We have lost enough time to him."

Anna shifted on her seat, nibbling at her muffin before she turned to Jeremiah. That they had both been praying through this was evident. She also knew that God was directing their steps along a path that he had already ordained for them to walk. He had never forsaken them no matter how many times that they had felt that way.

"I am not sure about that, Jeremiah. How can we?" Anna tamped down her fears as well as her dreams. "We're not the same people that we were."

"No, we are not. Life has changed us. Who knows who we would be if we had married all those years ago. God had this planned for us. He has allowed it for His plans and purposes. He is also here with us, directing our steps." Jeremiah reached to hug his lady, a kiss dropped on her temple. "So, what would you say if we were to marry today? You need someone to look after you."

Anna stared at him for a moment, seeing the love that he felt for her in his eyes and then the twinkle of mischief in his eyes. This was what she would have expected from the old Jeremiah. The new Jeremiah, the one who had returned after all those years, would not have approached her that way.

"I don't know what to say." She watched as his hand found hers once more and the ring that he had given her all those years ago was once more slipped on her finger. "Jeremiah? What do we tell my family?"

"That we still love one another and want to grow old together." Jeremiah sighed as he studied the parking lot outside of the car. He sensed that danger was around them. He just couldn't see who it was. "We need to move, love, but I don't want to pressure you."

"You're not." Anna bit at her lip as she prayed through her decision. "Okay. Let's do this as the boys would say. Today?"

"Today." Jeremiah drove away from that parking lot towards another town. "We'll find you your dress that you dreamed of, love. I know the minister from this town. He has been counselling me over the past few weeks. I didn't want to go to someone in our town."

"No, that wouldn't work. They would have let something slip." Anna was troubled by that. She knew that their own minister would not have but there were others who would. And Jeremiah didn't need that. Anna stopped her thoughts, blocking off the ones that said she needed her family there. She felt too dangerous for that. She just prayed that they would forgive her when they found out.

Standing in the bridal shop with her eyes trained on the gown that the saleslady had hung on the back of the change room door, Anna was very troubled. She didn't know if they were making the right move at all. She did not have the peace about it that she should have. And that peace was integral to her walk of life. Anna turned with a deep sigh of regret. She could not do this today. She could not marry Jeremiah that day. God had not given her permission to do so. And that permission and peace were what she needed to know in order to move ahead with the plans.

—

Anna reached for her purse, pausing to pray before she walked out of the room and then out of the shop, bypassing where she knew that Jeremiah was waiting for her. She hated to do that but she had to. Her phone was out as she called for a taxi. Once in the taxi and heading home, Anna sent a simple text message to Jeremiah, asking for his forgiveness and simply stating that they didn't have God's permission or blessing to go ahead with their plans.

Jeremiah stared in disbelief at the text message before he nodded. Anna was correct. They did need that. He sighed. Jeremiah was fully aware that Anna would have found a way home without letting him know. That's not who that she had been, but it was who she was now.

Chapter 28

Arlyn, Briar, and Cayce walked towards where their aunt was waiting for them, standing outside of a favourite restaurant, one that she had taken them to since they were small. The three men exchanged a glance with one another, not sure why Anna had asked to meet with them there. She had a reason, they knew, and at some point, she would talk with them.

Anna watched the triplets as they walked towards her, step in step and matching in height and looks. She thanked God that He had protected them and brought them through their difficulties successfully and with the life partners that He had chosen for them. However, Anna had decided that it was now time to go on the offensive. She had spent time on a phone call with Joe, going over everything, hearing his thoughts or as much as he could share. Anna had been open with him, giving him the name that had been uttered in her presence and what she knew of the man and his family. Joe had not really been surprised at the name. Anna had set her phone aside after the call just to spend time in prayer. She needed that time with her Heavenly Father and to feel the touch of His hand. Things were only going to get worse for her and Jeremiah and yes, she had to acknowledge as well, her family.

Hugging her nephews, Anna suddenly felt a sense of deep fear for them. She studied the pedestrians that were walking by them without seeing someone who would want to harm her. But someone was out there and nearby, that much she knew.

Seated in their favourite booth, the young men teased their aunt and then reminisced about the times that they had eaten there with her. It had been many. Anna was only about twelve years older than the triplets, Ardan and Bessie becoming parents in their very early twenties. She was more of a sister to them than an aunt at times.

Cayce finally reached for his aunt's hand, stopping the restless movement of it. His finger touched the ring on her hand.

"Aunt Anna? What's this?" He shared a look with the other two.

"It's Jeremiah's ring, yes. We are talking at present. For now, it's here. It may not stay." Anna was troubled at having to confess that. She had prayed hard before she had left it in place. God had not told her to remove it. Instead, she had a sense that it had to stay.

"You are? Does Dad know?" Briar spoke up at that point. He really wasn't sure about Jeremiah any more. As a youngster, he had looked up to him. Briar still wasn't sure if the story that Jeremiah was telling was the actual truth.

"He is. We've talked and prayed it through, boys." Anna sighed. "Jeremiah wanted to marry me one day last week. I walked out of the bridal shop. I just couldn't do it. God has not given me permission to marry yet. That may never come."

Arlyn nodded. He knew what his aunt was saying was how God worked. He also knew that his aunt was in close enough communication with their Heavenly Father to sense when that time would be right, if it ever was.

"What can we do for you, Aunt Anna?" Briar shared another look with his brothers.

"I really don't know at the moment, Briar. I need you to stay safe. And I just don't know how to manage that." Anna sighed as she saw the man whom she suspected of being behind it all stand and walk away. She felt the sudden fear that ran through her. That man meant harm to both herself and Jeremiah. She just didn't know how to stop him from harming them.

"Abe and Emma have been in touch." Arlyn wasn't sure how to proceed with what he needed to say.

"I know. They've reached out to me and also to Joe. And yes, Joe and I have talked." Anna sighed to herself. God, where are You? I know You are in control and hiding us all under the shadow of Your wings. It would be nice to have this resolved today but it is in Your timing, not ours.

"What can we do for you, Aunt Anna?" Cayce shared a look with his brothers, not sure what to say or even what help that they could give their aunt.

"I don't know, Cayce. I know that you and the girls have been working on this. How be we get together this week and see where we stand? And yes, Abe and Emma have been involved as has Blackie and that group." Anna didn't want to see her nephews injured in any way but she knew that they would not stay back from helping her. She had to let them.

"That works, Aunt Anna. How about Saturday at our place?" Briar knew that Brynne wanted this as much as he did. Neither one of them or any of Anna's family for that matter wanted to see her suffer more than she had. Not even Ardan and Bessie had known the burden that she had carried for so many years.

Anna nodded, her eyes and attention on the man who sat near them. She felt fear and almost terror as she watched him. She knew that he was aware that Anna was in the restaurant. Sudden fear drove through her, fear for her beloved nephews and their families. What would this man do to them? That was a question that Anna had no answer for and she didn't know who to ask, other than to beg God to protect her family.

Walking away from their aunts, the triplets shared a look. This was where it began to get very dangerous for her and also Jeremiah. They had seen the ring on her finger. They just weren't sure what that meant and hadn't felt as if they would even ask her.

"What do you think?" Arlyn finally had to ask. He knew that God was there and was protecting Anna. He just wanted in on that protection detail.

"I don't know what to think, guys." Briar rubbed at his face. "We need to do some work before them." His phone was out as it chimed. He frowned at the text message. "Emma sending us some stuff as she calls it and she asked if we were meeting on Saturday. How does she know?"

"It's Emma. We all know that is how she does it." Cayce frowned for a moment as he studied a message from Blackie. "And Blackie and Simon are heading our way on Saturday as well. Aunt Anna may not like it."

"She'll accept it because she knows they care. Now, do we involve Jeremiah as well?" Arlyn wasn't sure on that. His phone was out as he sent a quick message off to Anna, who responded that it was up to them if Jeremiah was there. She had no strong feelings either way. "That's strange, you know. She's wearing Jeremiah's ring again but she really doesn't seem as if she's engaged."

"No, she doesn't. It's been that long for her." Briar sighed. "Talk to Dad and see what his feelings are. I would say Jeremiah needs to be there, but I am not making that decision. One of the older adults who know him better need to do that."

Cayce began to grin, holding up his phone.

"Dad's weighed in. Aunt Anna had texted him. He wants Jeremiah there and will approach him." Cayce sighed. "I hate this. We know what we went through. I can't imagine how they feel after being apart for so many years." His brothers had to agree with him on that.

Chapter 29

Saturday found Ardan's house almost too full and overflowing with people. He stood in the kitchen doorway, listening to the conversations and laughter that filled his home. He smiled, albeit a sad smile. It should be a happy occasion but it wasn't. That distressed him to no end. Ardan looked up as he felt a hand on his shoulder. His friend, Samuel, stood there, a hand resting on his shoulder.

"Ardan? How are you in all of this?" Samuel suspected what the answer would be but he waited patiently for his friend to respond.

Ardan shrugged. Others had asked him that very question. He had no answer. He stared at the light yellow walls of the hallway, lost in thought for a moment.

"I don't know how to answer that question, Samuel. I really don't. It was one thing when it was my sons. For it to be my sister? And to have gone on for so long?" Ardan struggled with his emotions even as his socked foot rubbed at the dark oak flooring under it.

"That's fair, Ardan. It is different when it is your sister. You worry about her differently and always will. You two are close, that much I know. But I suspect there is much that she is keeping from you." Samuel gave a grim smile as he saw Anna watching them, a frown on her face.

"There is. She hasn't spoken a lot over the years of what went on around the time that Jeremiah disappeared. I know that she has been uncomfortable at times but has refused to speak." Ardan watched as his sister disappeared towards his office, a sigh rising from him. "How do we do this, Samuel? How do we solve this and then reconcile all of us? This is causing a rift in our family that was never there."

"And it will continue to do so, Ardan. I can't tell you what to do or what to say. That is between you and Anna. It is also between you and God. I know how strong your faith is. Just remember that God has never left either one of you or even Jeremiah. He has protected that couple over the years in ways we may never know about. A friend has a saying that God has plans and purposes for us that we don't understand and may never know about here on earth. Murphy is so right in that. And God is working in this. He has covered both Anna and Jeremiah with His hand and sheltered them from death more than likely." Samuel didn't let on that he had spoken with Jeremiah on many occasions in the last couple of months with Jeremiah and that man had shared what he had gone through. That had helped to drive the investigation forward.

"I get that, Samuel. I just don't like what Anna is going through." Ardan sighed as he felt Bessie's arm around him. "We are praying for them. It's just hard to know how to pray." He walked away, leaving Bessie staring after him, tears sparkling in her eyes.

"Bessie?" Samuel wished that Miriam had been able to make the trip with him that day but other commitments had prevented that.

"Ardan doesn't know what Anna and I have spoken about over the years. It was done in confidence, and I will not break that. Anna has been hurting for so many years. In the last couple of weeks, she sold her home and bought a condo. Ardan doesn't know where. She has not told him just to protect him. And she needs to. She has changed her appearance and what she does and eats. She has lived for over twenty years as she thought she should, just because it was what Jeremiah liked or what they had decided on as a couple. Anna told me that she had to take back her life and live it for herself even at this stage in her life. And that she and Jeremiah were talking but there was no firm decision on what they wanted to do." Bessie watched her sons and their wives as they mingled with the group. "She is that worried about the boys and their families. She hasn't said but I would suspect that they have been threatened."

"And she has given no clear answer as to why?" Samuel shook his head. "That will come and I fear for them, Bessie. Come. Let's spend some time in prayer and then look at what all everyone has found." He looked around as the door opened and Joe appeared. "Joe? You're here?"

"I am." Joe gave a quick grin. "As a friend today, not an investigator. If anything comes up that I need to do that with, I'll set it aside until Monday. I am under strict orders to do that." Joe hugged Bessie and then walked towards Ardan's office.

"He's a good man, Samuel, and has worked so hard on everything in the last couple of years."

"He has. Now, let's find our places and get this show on the road, as they say." Samuel walked away, leaving Blackie to stand beside Bessie.

"Bessie? What can we do for you?" He waited patiently for Bessie to speak. Instead she just walked away, leaving him with a small grin on his face. They would talk at some point, he knew.

Anna looked up as their time of prayer ended. She was grateful for everyone gathered there but also very afraid. She hadn't told anyone of the letter that she had found on her windshield that morning. The threats had been dire and downright evil. Anna knew that she needed to approach Joe. She just didn't want to.

Walking away from Ardan's house that afternoon, Anna was puzzled by the information that had been presented. She knew that it had been confirmed and that Joe would continue his own investigation into it. She had just not been prepared to hear that the man they all thought was the ringleader behind Jeremiah's imprisonment was in fact not that leader. There was someone behind him and that name frightened her very much.

Jeremiah paced beside her, his eyes worried as he studied Anna. He was so afraid that she would die because of him and that he could not bear to even think about.

"Anna?" His hand on her arm stopped her forward walk.

"What?" Anna's response was abrupt before she stopped and apologized. "I'm sorry. You didn't deserve that."

"No, I didn't but I get it. What are your thoughts?"

"My thoughts? I don't really know what to think. I have to think this through and study the information. That isn't happening today." Anna looked up at him, seeing the worry in his eyes. "You can't stop what's happening, Jeremiah. Only God can and He has not done that yet."

"No, He hasn't. Can we get together in the next couple of days? I want to hear your thoughts." Jeremiah frowned as she snorted. "Anna?"

"My thoughts? I don't know that you will want to hear them." Anna stopped walking abruptly, Jeremiah's hand slipping from her arm. She listened to the late afternoon sounds in the neighbourhood and then looked up. The sky was rapidly becoming cloud covered, angry dark clouds that foretold of a thunderstorm. "We need to let this sit for a couple of days, Jeremiah. Call me in three days. Not before." Anna walked away at that point, her stride angry yet showing her hurt and fear.

Jeremiah watched the love of his life walk away, fearing greatly for her safety and her life. He didn't want her to fall into the hands of that man. She would never survive. He stared down at the keys that he was holding, not sure where to turn other than to God. And he had been doing that. It was just that at times he didn't feel God's presence or think that God was hearing him even though he knew better.

Chapter 30

Dropping her phone to the table, Anna's hands covered her mouth as she stifled the scream that welled inside her. Her face paled as she listened to the vile threat that came over her phone. She just didn't understand how that person had retrieved her phone number. It was a private number and not out there for public retrieval.

Anna scrambled away from her kitchen, her eyes on the table and the phone. She had no clue who the voice belonged to. That voice simply threatened her. She didn't recognize it.

Turning as she heard the buzzer to the door, Anna reached for the video screen. Cayce and Haley stood there, waiting almost impatiently for her to let them in. She hit the button to release the door before she was back in the kitchen, her phone tucked away out of sight. Anna sighed as she walked to open the door. There was no way that she could hide this from the couple.

Cayce hugged his aunt before he stood back, a frown on his face.

"Aunt Anna? What happened?" Cayce waited almost impatiently for her to respond. "What did you get?"

"A voice message. I just listened to it before you rang to get in." Anna refused to hand over her phone despite Cayce's hand going out for it. "No, Cayce. I'll contact Joe but I am not letting you listen to it. You had enough with your own adventure."

Cayce gave a brief grin. She was correct, he knew, but he worried about his aunt.

"We need to protect you, Aunt Anna. How do we do that?" Cayce shared a look with Haley who had turned from the counter. "And we are not walking away from you, not at all."

"You need too, all of you, but I know that you won't. Now, what were you doing coming here?" Anna reached for the kettle, intent on making them tea.

"We just needed to see you." Haley hugged Anna. "We also wanted your thoughts on what was discussed the other day. And we're not leaving until we have those." She grinned at her aunt by marriage.

"You're not? And if I refuse to give them?" Anna grinned at Haley before she turned to retrieve her notes from the office. "I do have thoughts and I do appreciate you two coming here." She sighed as the door buzzer sounded again. "Now who?"

Briar, Brynne, Arlyn, and Skylor stared at Anna as she stared back at them. She hadn't expected all of them to show up but she should have. The only one missing was Jeremiah and she knew that he had appointments all day that would keep him away. Or at least that was what she thought.

"What are we looking at?" Anna studied each one of the younger people. "What have you six discovered? And don't tell me nothing. I know better than that."

The six younger folk grinned at her before Arlyn reached to hug his aunt. He was deeply afraid for her.

"We have discovered something that we need to discuss. Only, I'm not sure how to broach the subject." Arlyn bit at his lip.

"What did you discover, Arlyn?" Anna reached for the pile of folders that she had dropped on the table. "Let's head into the living room and see how the discussion goes. I am interested to see what you have discovered."

Three hours later, Anna looked at the clock and rose, heading to the kitchen. They needed to eat but the younger people also needed to head for their young families. The six had spent hours trying to determine just what and who was after Jeremiah and after Anna. Briar was convinced that whoever had imprisoned Jeremiah had been after Anna and this was one way to destroy her life. Only that had not worked out.

Anna had listened to them all, particularly Briar. She knew him well enough to see how troubled he was with his thoughts. She hugged them all, sent them on their way, and then found her seat in the living room once more. Anna ignored the time and the fact that she should be eating to re-read what their conclusions were. She nodded. Briar was on the right track, she decided, as she reached for her phone. Joe had sent a text message, just asking to meet with her that day. She replied that she couldn't and would the next day do. She just didn't have it in her to meet with him that day.

Jeremiah set his phone to one side and reached for his Bible instead. He needed that time with his Heavenly Father just to be reminded of how much he was loved and protected. He could feel the walls closing in on him again and hated that. Jeremiah also worried about Anna. It was one thing to have worried about her when he was a prisoner and unable to do anything. It was another to be free and in the same city. He sighed. Jeremiah knew that he was doing God's work for him, worrying about the love of his life. He couldn't help himself. He turned instead to God's word, immersing himself in the promises of peace in times of trials, protection, and mercy. He frowned as he studied the verses for mercy, knowing that he had to show that towards his enemies. That was one thing that Jeremiah didn't want to do but knew that he had to fight it out and extend that at some point.

Briar turned to Brynne late that night, wrapping her into his arms. He waited for her to speak. When she didn't, he leaned back to look down at her.

"Brynne?"

"Briar, what are we to do? This is getting so dangerous for your aunt and for us as well. Whoever it is will go after us, won't they if they can't get to Aunt Anna?" Brynne expressed what Briar had been thinking and what he knew his brothers were thinking as well.

"They may, love. They may. We need to be aware of what is around us at all times. We know that feeling only too well."

"We do. I'm afraid for the little ones. What if they come after one of them?"

"I don't know that they will. We'll watch our little ones as carefully as we can. If they are going to go after any of us, I would say it would be Arlyn or Cayce. Or even Dad. That would hurt both Aunt Anna and Jeremiah." Briar had a sinking feeling in the pit of his stomach that what he had described would actually happen.

Chapter 31

Standing on her balcony, Anna stared at the sky over Lake Erie. The dark clouds were gathering rapidly. She could hear the gradually louder rumbles of thunder and the increasing flashes of lightning. A thunderstorm was moving in and that she didn't like. Thunderstorms never used to bother her but the ones lately had been. She put that down to the stress in her life that was driving her emotions into a whirlwind.

Anna had spent over half an hour on a call with Joe, just going back over what had happened when Jeremiah had vanished and anything that might have come out of that disappearance over the years. Joe was particularly interested in what was happening in the last few weeks. Anna had finally told him that he had picked her brain clean and she didn't know what else that she could tell him. He hadn't liked that. Joe was sure that there was just that one little detail that was missing. He was not happy when Anna finally told him enough was enough and hung up on him. That she was in a very dangerous situation? He had tried to get through to her but it didn't seem that he had.

Thinking through what Joe had asked and then stated, Anna's fear was growing rapidly. She was being followed everywhere she went. Her fear was that one of the boys, one of their wives, or one of the little ones would be hurt. She didn't know if she could live with that. Anna had finally had to turn that worry and fear over to God. That was all that she could do.

He was in control and that she had to acknowledge and accept.

She turned away from the balcony, not seeing the man who had his gaze trained on her. He had tried to get into the building but had been blocked from that. He was under orders to bring Anna to his boss and do it in the next two days. He just didn't know how he was going to be able to do that. She just wasn't on her own at any point.

Early morning found Anna back on her balcony, watching as the sun began its early morning peeking over the horizon. She turned and tied on her sneakers and then found her keys. She just needed to be out in the early morning. Anna ran down the stairs that led to the outside, the heavy metal door closing behind her. Her feet carried her towards the beach that lay across from the condo building.

Unaware of the danger that lurked in the darkness and half light of a new day, Anna walked the beach. Her face was raised to the faint breeze that was blowing inland from the lake. Her heart was raised in petition that whatever was going on ended soon. Anna didn't hear the faint sounds of the sand being disturbed by running feet.

A hand across her mouth choked off her scream as an arm wrapped itself around her, trapping hers to her torso. She was picked up and bodily carried away from the beach and then dumped into the backseat of a truck. Anna fought to escape her attacker to no avail. She struggled to identify him with no success. Anna didn't realize that another man was behind her until she felt the prick of a needle and her struggles gradually ceased. The first man gulped in air. He had not expected Anna to fight him as she had.

Anna was carried from the truck and dumped in a very small, barren room. She didn't rouse at all as the door was locked behind the men. It would be hours before she would rouse and then try to find a way out of the room. Only, there was no way out. She was now a prisoner, just by whom and why, she could not determine.

Jeremiah searched the small restaurant where Anna was to have met him before he searched outside of it. There was no sign of her. His calls and text messages went unanswered. Reaching out to Ardan, he was unable to contact him. Jeremiah turned as he heard someone calling his name.

Joe paused as he caught the frantic way that Jeremiah was pacing, His eyes closed for a moment. Anna must be missing.

"Joe? Have you talked with Anna today?" Jeremiah was praying that he had. His heart sank as Joe shook his head.

"Have you?" Joe waited somewhat impatiently for Jeremiah to respond. All he could do was pray for his friend.

"No. We were to meet and she hasn't shown." Jeremiah was almost in panic mode as Joe drew him to one side. "I can't reach her family."

Joe looked around, feeling them being watched. He pulled Jeremiah with him as he headed for his car and almost shoved the older man inside before he sped away, intent on tracking Anna down.

By early evening, it was obvious that Anna was indeed missing. No one had seen her since the previous day. The three boys paced the beach across from her home, their eyes on her condo.

"Where is she?" Arlyn spoke for the three of them.

"I wish that I knew. I would bring her home." Briar walked away from his brothers, not sure where he should be. He could only pray for his aunt.

Anna didn't rouse as the lock sounded in the door and then the door opened. Heavy footsteps sounded across the floor as her captor stood over her. He nodded. He finally had her where he wanted her and she would never return to her family. Anna was to be used to bring Jeremiah to him and then they would both die. It was long overdue.

Arlyn turned three days later. He had slipped out in the early morning, seeking to find his aunt. His hands raised in the air as he saw the weapon pointed at him. As hard as he tried, Arlyn could not identify anything distinguishing about the man in front of him. Forced into a vehicle, Arlyn flinched as a blindfold was dropped over his eyes and then he felt the rope that bound his hands. He could hear the early morning sounds of nature as well as the early morning traffic.

Pulled from the vehicle, Arlyn stumbled as he was forced to walk forward. He could not distinguish anything that would help him determine where he was. The rope was cut from his wrists before the door was slammed behind him and silence reigned in the room other than for his ragged breathing,

Arlyn pulled the blindfold from his face and stared at the sparsely furnished room. He had no idea where he was or who was his captor. Fear welled within him as he prayed for release and then for safety for his family.

Chapter 32

Skylor paced their home that evening. Arlyn had not appeared for their supper and there had neen no word from him all that day. She had contacted the family. No one had seen him or spoken with him.

Joe shut the door quietly behind him and he watched Skylor cuddle the little one tightly to her.

"You have not had any word since we spoke this afternoon?" Joe was worried about his friend. Word on the street was that Anna's family was at risk. Jeremiah had not been able to provide any assistance or answers when questioned.

"None. And that is not him." Skylor was becoming more worried.

"Let me take you to Ardan's. At least for the night." Joe worked to help pack what would be needed. Abe had reached out to him in the last hour and offered his team to help search for Arlyn. The two men had talked, expressing their fear that the other two nephews would disappear as well.

Ardan and Bessie stared at Joe as he helped Skylor into their home. What they had feared had happened. One of their sons had disappeared again. God was in control, they knew. It didn't make it any easier.

Arlyn paced the room that he was locked into. He had no idea who had taken him captive but he suspected that it had to do with Jeremiah. He wanted that man in front of him at that time to answer what the reason was for his abduction. Arlyn didn't know if he was the only one who was held captive there. He had been unable to determine that and the walls were too thick for him to hear anyone else. All he could do was beg God for release and then beg God to keep his wife and baby safe.

Anna roused to some extent, hearing footsteps in the room with her. She lay still, her eyes closed but her senses alert to the man standing over her. She had no idea who he was or what he wanted. All she could do was rest in the promises that God would protect her.

Two days later, Briar was carried to another room in the hallway, across from the one that held his aunt. He had been approached on his lunch hour and he had fought the men trying to take him captive. A lucky blow from one of the men had knocked him out and that had aided the two men in bringing him to the house where they would meet the man responsible for Jeremiah's captivity and for having their aunt monitored for so many years.

Brynne was scared and fled as well to Ardan's home. Joe had reached out to her, but he had no answers as to where Briar was or who was responsible. He was now worried that Cayce would also disappear. Cayce had simply shrugged and stated that God was in control.

Abe appeared the next day, worried about his friends. He had been in contact with two undercover officers from their town, Will and Bob. There was no word on the streets as to why the three had disappeared or where they were. That worried Abe to no end. He needed to find them and had no idea where to look.

Emma was desperately searching for them but finding no information as to where they might be. That was highly unusual for her.

Joe had talked with Jeremiah. Neither man could get a grip on what was happening. Joe had eyed Jeremiah, certain that he had an idea as to who it was other than the names that he had provided to Joe. Jeremiah had shaken his head and then walked away to find his prayer corner and beg God to protect the three.

Four days later, Haley turned to speak with Cayce, finding him not where she expected him to be. She searched their home and yard, fearing that he too had disappeared. Her fear seemed to be true. She packed up the twins and what they would need and headed for her in-laws, letting her father and brother know that Cayce had now disappeared and where she would be.

Ardan stared at the three young ladies as they huddled together. Enough was enough, he decided. They needed to find his family. He just didn't know how to. He reached out to Samuel and through him to Blackie and Simon. Surely, they could find out some sort of information for them.

Joe stared at Ardan as he informed him that Cayce was missing as well. He shook his head before he walked away. When did it end, he wondered? He had no idea where the four were. And Jeremiah didn't seem to know either. Joe knew that Emma was racing to find what information that she could but even Emma seemed to have hit a roadblock. Joe prayed that they were still in town and still alive. He didn't want to be the one to break that kind of news to the young wives.

———

Early the next morning, Joe turned from the counter at a local diner, a cup of coffee in his hand. He was exhausted and frustrated, He was no further ahead in his search for the four. He paused for a moment as he stood beside his car, parked behind the diner. He heard a whisper of sound barely audible above the noise of the traffic before a body slammed into him and took him to the pavement. Joe struggled mightily to get the upper hand on his opponent. He just didn't see the second man appear and slam a weapon barrel against Joe's head. Joe collapsed, leaving the man he was fighting with to gasp for air before he reached for Joe's police gear and dumped it into Joe's car, including the small beacon that was even then sending out a warning that Joe was down and not moving.

Alarm spread through the precinct as officers including David scrambled when word spread that Joe's beacon was going off. Consternation spread through the officers as they searched for Joe without finding him. They were all puzzled at finding the police gear in Joe's car. There was just no explanation for that.

David stood back from the scene, a thoughtful look on his face. He nodded at last. Joe had to have been taken by the same people who had taken the Koyles. He just didn't understand it.

Joe was dragged into the same building as the others, a door closing and locking behind him. His body lay on the floor, blood slowly trickling from the wound on his head. The man was satisfied. He had the ones that he needed. The next step was to draw out Jeremiah and get him back under his control. He was confident that this would work. He just didn't reckon on Who he was dealing with. God was in control of the situation. It was only by His will and grace that the five were locked into that building. God would not allow anything to happen to them that was not in His will or plan for them.

Consternation spread among the Koyles before they looked at one another and dove deeper into their research. Abe and Emma were frequent visitors as were Samuel, Blackie, and Simon. Richard and Don, other friends with security teams, had been around, not only to help investigate but also to search. The streets were quiet. No one seemed willing or able to help. That puzzled them all. Even Will and Bob could not find any information on the five.

Chapter 33

Jeremiah turned from the front window in his home, listening as Carl and Greg discussed the situation with Abe, Don, and Richard. None of them had any idea of where to start their search or even who to look for. The man who had held Jeremiah captive for so long had been found dead in his home, the victim of a murder. That ended that part of it for Jeremiah, or did it? He was convinced that the man was still alive and nothing that was said or details that were presented to him convinced him otherwise.

Abe and Richard approached Jeremiah, uncertain as to whether he had been completely honest with them. Abe studied the man, seeing the agitation and fear that he was trying hard to hide. He also heard the silence from the other men, knowing that they were waiting for Jeremiah to respond to their questions.

"Jeremiah, what makes you think that this man is still alive?" Richard's question caught Jeremiah's attention.

Jeremiah shrugged. He had no proof against what had been presented to him.

"He's too mean to die. And I saw him yesterday." His words stopped any questions that hovered in the air.

"You saw him?" Carl was on his feet, heading for Jeremiah.

"I did. He was standing on my lawn and was gone before I could even react. He has Anna and the boys. What does he want?"

"Revenge." Don was on his feet, heading for the front door as a tap came to it. He stood back to let Emma enter. "Emma?"

"Don? That man isn't dead. It was someone who resembled him. I just got confirmation of that." Emma waved a paper in the air. "He's here in town."

"Jeremiah just stated that." Abe reached for the paper, read it and then passed it on. "Now what?"

"Now what? We come up with a plan to find him. Jace is working on addresses. Naomi is working through his list of aliases. And he had many. We'll find him and find the others." Emma's gaze was sympathetic as she watched Jeremiah struggle with his emotions. She watched as the men's heads all bowed as they petitioned God for the safety of their friends.

"Jeremiah? Talk to us. Tell us everything that you know about this man." Richard turned to Carl and Greg. "And the same for you two."

Words flew among the men as they desperately searched for any place where the five were being held. Emma walked towards the door at one point, opening it to find both Ardan and David there. She watched as Ardan struggled with his emotions. Ardan shook his head at Emma before he stalked into the living room, to simply stand and watch and listen. His emotions were raw on his face.

_____

David spoke quietly with the three men he knew best. He was unsure how far that he could trust Carl and Greg. Somewhere there was a leak. He had spoken to Emma and she had agreed with his assessment. David studied the room, knowing from Joe that Jeremiah had moved houses and sold his childhood home. Neither officer was sure what the motivation had been or even if it had been a good idea. Jeremiah had looked at them when they questioned him and then walked away, leaving silence in his wake.

The four Koyle ladies were despairing that they would see any of the missing again. Skyler paced the sunroom, her attention not in the cream walls, dark floors, white wicker furniture, or the colourful jade and coral cushions. She was desperate to have Arlyn back home. She turned to the other ladies..

"How do we find them?" She sank down to the floor, her arms cuddling her young daughter.

"We are praying, Skylor. It is hard to wait and watch. This is where our faith comes in. We were prayed for in the garden all those years ago. God knew then what we would face." Bessie was trying to stay positive but was struggling. She blinked back her tears.

"It is hard." Brynne hugged her young son, clinging to him. She was terrified that Briar would die and she would be raising their son on her own.

"We will find them." Haley rose and left the room, returning with a stack of paper. Her brother had been around the night before, dropping off material that the group from The Barnabas Foundation has forwarded to him. "Josh dropped this off last night.

He said that they had found information for us. We go through it and talk to the others."

Jeremiah turned as he felt a hand touch his shoulder. Ardan stood there before he prayed for the man who claimed to love his sister. He nodded at the unspoken question in Ardan's eyes before the two men walked away and left the house.

"Ardan, where would you begin to search? I don't know this town anymore."

Ardan nodded. He had been trying to determine just where to start. His hand pulled Jeremiah with him as he almost ran for his car.

"We need to speak with Jake at the diner. He can help." Ardan sped away from the house, neither man noticing Don running for his car to follow them.

Jake nodded at the questions fired at him by Ardan. He pointed towards his office, waiting only to follow the two men to take time to grab a tray with mugs of coffee. Don simply walked after the other two and found his own chair in the office.

"Jake." Ardan's voice held hope.

"I know, Ardan. We need to pray first. Then we talk. Don? It will be up to you to discuss this with Richard and Abe and make plans. Word has reached me of a few properties where they may be. I am no certain which one."

Don nodded, knowing it was not the first time that Jake had assisted one of the security teams in finding missing persons.

Chapter 34

Jeremiah paced his home that night. He thought that they had come to some agreement as to who had them. It was someone behind that man as he was termed. Sighing to himself, Jeremiah found his prayer corner. Tonight would be one of those nights where he struggled with his faith and had to wait in silence for God to speak to him.

Ardan paced his home office. He was sorrowing not just for himself but for his family. He had watched the young wives that night, seeing how they trying to stay strong for each other but there was coming realization that the triplets may not come home as they were praying and hoping for.

Early the next morning, Skylor opened the door and stared at Jeremiah. She stepped back to let him enter.

"You're here early." She headed for the kitchen and reached for the coffee pot even as she yawned.

"I am. Today? We need to refine our plans to bring everyone home." Jeremiah reached for the little girl in Skylor's arms, cuddling her to him.

Skylor stared at him. There was something different about him that morning, a confidence that she had not seen before. She didn't know that this was who he had been in the past.

"We do?   What information did you get overnight?"

"No new information. It has just become very clear." Jeremiah's body rocked slowly from side to side as the little girl cuddled close to the older man, surprising her mother. "Ardan and I talked with Jake yesterday. Don was there. I have had time to ruminate over that information and lay it out before God. God spoke, Skylor."

Skylor nodded. That was what God did.

"It's not your fault, Jeremiah. You have been carrying a huge load of grief, regret, and responsibility. You have released it, haven't you? We do need to meet. The guys from the Barnabas Foundation have been in touch and forwarded a lot of information. We need to collate what we ladies have with what you guys have. Don and Richard are to be here shortly. We're set up to work in the office. Haley named someone last night." Skylor nodded at the name that Jeremiah uttered. "That's who. We came to that conclusion last night. Haley knows her town. We just have to determine where he is. Emma sent through a number of addresses that he has. She's working on deciding which one." Skylor looked behind Jeremiah to see Ardan and Don standing there.

Ardan nodded to himself. Jeremiah was back. Now, to find his family. He considered Joe part of that.

"Let's find our coffee, Skylor, and then spend some time in prayer. We need to track down that man and do that today."

———

177

Don agreed. His security team was meeting with those of Richard and Abe. They would move in once an address was confirmed. That had already been confirmed with the police chief and a judge.

Four hours later, their heads raised as they heard the footsteps of some of the ladies. Ardan and Don were on their feet to take the trays of coffee, tea, and snacks that the ladies had prepared. They needed that break. Progress was being made but they still had addresses to rule out or confirm. Emma had appeared, working remotely to her office with Jace and Naomi.

"Have we made any progress?" Brynne thought that they had but wasn't sure.

"We have, Brynne." Don was quick to reassure her. "We have made progress. God is leading us to where your family is. We'll find them and bring them home." He was confident on that. He had been in and out of the discussions over the morning, in constant contact with Abe and Richard who were scouring the town with the three teams. They were confident that within the next twenty-four hours they would confirm the address where the family was being held and be able to go in and find them. They just worried about what condition the family would be in. Joe they were sure had been hurt, just from the evidence that had been found. They were not sure about the triplets but once more evidence suggested that Brynne had fought his abductors and may have been hurt. That worried the three team leaders but their worry was hidden from the family. The family didn't need to know that until their family members were at home.

———

Jeremiah paced his home once more that night. One of Don's men, Paul, was with him. They have felt it necessary to bring in someone to be with him. He had been against him, not wanting to put anyone else at risk. Paul had shrugged, pointed to his car, and drove Jeremiah to his home. What Jeremiah didn't know what that others from the three teams were situated outside of his home, watching out for him. Will and Bob had reached out to Jake who in turn had reached out to Don and alerted him to the fact that Jeremiah was to disappear that night. They were there to ensure that didn't happen.

Retiring at last, Ardan worried more than he had about his sister and his sons and Joe. He was so afraid, almost terrified, that they would be holding funerals for them instead of welcoming them back into their families. He had watched the three younger ladies that day, seeing how they were struggling to stay strong and at times dissolving into tears. Bessie had also tried her best to stay strong but had disappeared at times, coming back into the group with tear-drenched and reddened eyes. All Ardan could do was hug her and then turn back to their research.

Richard pocketed his phone in the early morning hours. He was on his feet and searching for Abe and Don, finding them with their heads bent as they prayed. He joined them, waiting until their prayers were over before he spoke.

"Jake has been in touch." Richard shared a look with the two men. "He knows where they are."

"And he has given you that address?" Don reached for the piece of paper that Richard held. As he read it, he frowned. "That's near Jeremiah's."

"It is. He wants to be close so that he can watch the devastation that he expects Jeremiah to show. Only, Jeremiah is not doing that. None of them are. Their faith is being tested but they are staying strong in God."

Chapter 35

Abe stood in the shadows of the trees, his gaze focused on the box-like house across the street from where he, Don, and Richard had gathered. He was well aware that their three teams were somewhere nearby, just waiting for word to move in. He squinted as he glanced towards the sky. It was early morning and they needed to move in soon. He heard quiet footsteps and turned to face the lead of the emergency response team as he approached, geared up and ready to move in.

"All set?" Abe kept his voice low.

"We are. Your teams are ready?" Ted looked around, seeing four men moving in to flank Abe.

"They are. These four men go in with us. They're with the men. I am with Anna."

Moving quickly, the officers headed for the doors to the house, the five men from the security teams behind them. Surprised to find the doors unlocked, the men entered, yelling that they were the police and for whoever was there to come out with their hands raised. Shocked to find the house empty, the search was on to find the captives.

Ted turned to Abe as they entered a narrow hallway lined with locked doors.

"This is strange, Abe. What is going on?"

"These are a type of cell. We've seen it before. Let's get the doors open. I suspect the rooms will be very basic." Abe turned for a moment as he heard loud commotion from outside, catching the nod that Ted gave. He sighed. There just had to be him show up. He prayed that they got them all and that this was over for the Koyles. Somehow though he didn't think that it was.

Reaching for the keys that had remained in the locks, the officers quickly opened the doors. They were greeted with surprised looks on the faces of the four young men. The triplets were rushed away, able to manage on their own. Joe hesitated for a moment before hands reached to help him. He had been treated rougher than the others just because he was an officer.

Abe was on his knees beside Anna who had not responded at all to the opening door. He looked up and nodded at Ted before he gathered Anna up into his arms and headed for the outdoors and the waiting paramedics.

The young men watched as Abe emerged, fear in their hearts for Anna. They knew that she had been failing in the last couple of days but they had been prevented from helping her. They were quickly assessed and then removed from the area, a security team member and police officer with each one.

Abe gently placed Anna on a stretcher and then stood with his back to her, monitoring the area around them. He could hear the muted conversation of the paramedics, a worried tone to their voices.

Sudden hurried commotion and shouts drew his attention to a small building off to one side. Officers were running that way before the emergency response team sniper fired only one shot. A man tumbled from the roof to the ground where he didn't move. Abe drew in a deep breath. That had been too close. He was up and into the paramedic rig and finding a corner to tuck himself away in, his eyes on Anna. Anna had not yet responded and that worried him.

Don and Richard walked quickly towards the teams, sorting out who went where. They themselves were heading for Ardan's home, a police escort in place.

Ardan stared at Don, not sure that he had heard him correctly. His mouth opened and closed without a sound being heard. His head began to shake in a negative manner.

"That can't be right. You can't have found them." Ardan felt Bessie's hand on his back and her soft sobs.

"We have, Ardan. Let's get you to your family. Richard's team is moving in here for now for the children. We will get them to you but for now, the two ladies and the men on his team will protect the little ones. Of the men will be here. That way you can concentrate on what you need to." Don watched with sympathy on his face as the younger ladies scrambled to sort out what they needed to before they were running for the waiting vans. Ardan had hesitated, tears on his cheeks as he raised his face to thank their Heavenly Father. He didn't know what condition his family was in, but they were free.

———

183

"I was able to reach Joe's parents. The pilot for the Barnabas Foundation is on his way back with them. Barnabas can contact him."

Richard and Don shared a deep look. They had spoken with Barnabas already and he had been relieved to hear that the five were as safe as they could be. They all knew that it was not over for the five, not while the captors were still out there.

Pacing aimlessly as they waited for word on their loved ones, Ardan and Jeremiah didn't speak. They were begging God for relief that the five were not injured in any way. Neither Richard nor Don had said, knowing it was not their place to do so.

The triplets were soon on their feet and headed for their ladies, wrapping them in their arms as they sobbed. Their parents wrapped each couple in hugs as they were prayed for. The attention then returned to the doors to the ward as they waited on word on Joe and Anna.

David studied Joe carefully, concerned about the concussion he had obtained. Joe would not be on duty for the foreseeable future and that was not what David needed to hear. Besides that, Joe was a victim of crime and needed counselling for that as did the others.

"Talk to me, Joe. Tell me what happened."

Joe nodded. He had given his statement but he still needed to go over in detail what had transpired.

"It was bizarre, David, how they would bring us out each day. Anna was made to sit in a chair in the middle of an empty room. Us guys had to stand against a wall. We were not allowed to look at one another or speak. They were trying to break us. Except it didn't work."

185

Rousing hours later, Anna refused to open her eyes. She was convinced that she was still held captive. She just could not understand the soft sounds around her, the quiet footsteps, or the smells that were usually associated with a hospital. That she couldn't understand. Anna barely kept herself from jumping in fear as a hand rested on her hair before she heard Ardan praying for her. She felt his kiss on her cheek. Before she could respond, Arden's footsteps faded.

Anna shifted on the bed, sensing that she was not alone. A hand clasped hers before she heard Jeremiah praying for her and the boys and then heard his whispered words of love. He too kissed her forehead before he left.

Her eyes opening, Anna searched for the man who had held her captive. She didn't see him but she did see David waiting patiently for her to notice him.

"Anna? We need to get your statement. The boys have given theirs."

Anna nodded. She knew that she had to. She just didn't want to. Anna was also afraid for her family. They had been threatened. She knew the boys and Joe were there. She had seen them and that had terrified her.

"Where do I start?" Anna took with gratitude the glass of water that David handed her after he had raised the head of the bed. Anna had been moved to a private room with the door guarded by both officers and security personnel.

"The beginning, you say? Okay. The beginning it is. God protected us all. We were not harmed in any physical way during our captivity. I see the date that you are trying to hide. We know exactly how long each of us were held you. It was made a point to tell us each day." Anna sighed. She had no wish to relive her last few days but it was necessary. "It was Larry Waite that held. I recognized his voice even though we never saw his face. I can't describe the men. They ensured that seeing their faces didn't happen. For the most part, we were locked into those tiny rooms. There was a mattress on the floor, a couple of blankets, and a table by the door where our food for the day was dropped each morning. I had the basic washroom with a curtain around it. You saw the rooms. The light during the day was from a skylight and electric light during the night.

"Each day, at some point we were pulled from the rooms, walked downstairs and shoved into an empty room. I was forced to sit on a hard wooden chair facing away from the door. There were no windows and no other furnishings. The boys I think stood behind me against the wall. I could hear their footsteps as they entered the room. They were brought in one at a time after me and then led out one at a time before I was taken back to my cell. This was done to play with our minds. I hadn't slept and last night couldn't stay awake. Abe tells me that he carried me out when I didn't wake up."

David nodded as Anna finished her statement. It was about how he thought it had been.

"You have described what we thought happened. When you didn't break or cooperate with them? That's when they started bringing in the boys. That made no difference in how you reacted. We suspect if you had tried to escape or even to talk, you would have been treated harsher. Larry is in custody." David tucked away his pen and gathered his paperwork. "I understand that you are here overnight. We have guards at your door. Tomorrow we will get you together with your family."

Anna nodded, blinking back tears. God had released them but it was not over.

"The boys?"

"They are mostly physically okay. Briar was roughed up as he fought them. Joe had it the worst of them. They took him down while he was on duty. He has been dealing with a concussion. The ladies and the little ones headed for Ardan and Bessie when their guys disappeared." David looked towards the door. "Jeremiah is waiting outside. I am sending him in. We need to keep you two together for now." He walked away as Anna's mouth opened to protest, a prayer rising for a quick resolution to this.

Anna watched the door close, a sob rising within her. This was not over, she knew. The ones responsible were still out there and this time, Anna knew that neither Jeremiah nor herself would walk away. She didn't hear the door swish open or the quiet footsteps that approached her. Anna jumped as she felt arms surround her and hug her tightly. The quiet prayer that Jeremiah uttered broke through the tight control of her emotions and she wept. Jeremiah could only hold his beloved Anna, pray for her, and weep as well.

Chapter 37

The next morning, Anna stood in Ardan's kitchen and listened to the various conversations that were going on. Jeremiah's arms were around her and she leaned back on him. Anna wanted this over and over now. Jeremiah had bared his heart to her the night before in a way that he hadn't before. Anna had simply hugged him and agreed to his request. A beautiful white wedding dress now hung in her closet. Their plans were made and those plans included a small ceremony with just her family and of course Joe and his parents.

At the moment, however, Anna was determined to go through all the material that had been amassed and determine just who it was. She had to agree with Haley when Haley had approached her with that name. Jeremiah had stared at the two ladies, not quite sure that they were correct. He had then sighed. God was providing the name and would provide the needed proof.

Anna studied the material that had grown over the days. She knew that their friends were working to solve the answers to why it had happened but there was just one piece of evidence that was missing. Jeremiah moved with her, his arm around his beloved Anna. He was so afraid that he would lose her or that she would disappear for good. Neither one had a sense as to who the mastermind would be.

Arlyn bit at his lip before he approached his aunt. An arm came out to hug her even as he hesitated to speak. Anna's head tilted to watch him before she hugged him and then found a seat for them both to sit. Jeremiah was beside Anna, his arm around her once more.

"Arlyn? What have you discovered?" Anna waited patiently for Arlyn to gather his thoughts and then speak.

"Aunt Anna, hear me out. I have argued this out with Briar and Cayce. We are all in agreement. We don't think that it was Jeremiah totally. We think some of this has been directed at you. While Jeremiah was not here, you were safe. Now that he's back? Your danger level has increased. Who would want to harm you?" Arlyn watched his aunt closely, seeing her blink in surprise before she nodded.

"That's what we decided and have come to that conclusion, Arlyn. It has never made total sense. Sure, Jeremiah was targeted because of his skills with the jewels. But there has been something that just didn't sit right with all that." Anna looked up at Jeremiah, seeing his nod of comprehension. Her gaze took in the comfortable sage and cream of Ardan's office, with the dark oak furnishings and the full book shelves. "We need to figure out who."

Arlyn extended his hand, a piece of paper shaking slightly with the force of his emotions.

"We think it's this person, Aunt Anna. This person has been hiding well all these years even though we are now picking up rumours about him." Arlyn was not comfortable accusing the man, without all the evidence that would be needed. "Emma has approached us as well. She is working on finding the proof that we need.”

“And you haven’t gone to Joe or David as yet?” Jeremiah spoke up, knowing this to be the case.

“No, we haven’t. We wanted proof before we did so.” Cayce crouched down in front of his aunt. “Emma just sent word. She has forwarded the proof to Joe. We just need to figure out why he has been stalking you all these years.”

Anna sat back, feeling Jeremiah’s arm tightening on her. This is it, she thought. She began to pray, begging God for His protection and peace and assurance that they were not alone as they walked the final steps of this adventure, if that’s what it could be called. Anna was confident that God was there. He had allowed Jeremiah to return and be reunited with her, allowing them to move forward with plans from so many years ago.

“Emma has proof? Then we need to think about how we will draw him out.”

Jeremiah cleared his throat. He knew how to do it. He just wasn’t comfortable putting himself or Anna out there.

“He’ll be around on Saturday as we marry, sweetheart. He won’t stay away. Will and Bob have put out the word that’s what we’re doing.”

“I know.” Anna chewed at her lip, a new habit that she had picked up. “We’re not planning on living in your house for now. We have better security at the condo. It’s when we’re out and about.” She looked up as Briar approached them as well. "It's the triplets and their families that we need to worry about."

Briar was shaking his head. He didn't think that they needed to worry about their families even though they would be. The man was obsessed with harming their aunt. They just had to think of how to protect her.

"He won't go after us again. It didn't work before. He's not one to repeat something like this. He'll want to find you on your own." Briar held up papers that he had printed. "Emma has sent through this. We need to go through it and then make plans."

Anna reached for the paperwork, finding Jeremiah reading over her shoulder. She was not surprised by what Emma had discovered even though Jeremiah was. He paused on a paragraph, his finger pointing to it.

"He has these many homes? How do we narrow down which one he'll be in?"

"He'll be in the one that gives him the best access to you two." Cayce pointed to an address. "This one. It's close to here and to Jeremiah's home. He'll think that you two are going to live there. But you're not. You're in the condo. He doesn't have any property close to there. That throws off his plans."

Briar grinned for a moment. He had a plan but he didn't know how to express it. Arlyn studied him and then poked at his shoulder.

"What are you thinking, Briar?"

They listened closely to what Briar had thought of. Ardan frowned at his son and then suddenly grinned. It could very well work, he decided, sharing a look with Bessie. The younger ladies were not as sure as the older ones, Brynne expressing her opinion very forcefully.

Chapter 38

The next day, the Tuesday before their wedding, Anna and Jeremiah began their planned campaign to draw out the man behind it all. Anna had headed for her workplace, just to ask for an extended leave. With what she had gone through, she wasn't ready to go back to work. Her employer had looked at her and then nodded. He didn't want to lose her and if granting this request kept her as an employee, then he was ready to work with her.

Jeremiah had walked into the jewelry store and hunted for David. The newer and younger employees were not sure of his status there, not fully understanding what had transpired with Jeremiah. The older employees who knew Jeremiah had welcomed him back, content with what little he could tell them. Jeremiah had been missed.

David studied the man in front of him. He had planned to sell his store to Jeremiah at some point. Now, he was not sure that Jeremiah would stay. He had been the best jeweller that David had seen and even with his skills rusty, his designs were above any that David had seen.

"What are you saying, Jeremiah?"

"Anna and I are planning to marry on Saturday. We want you there. But between then and now, we are going on the offensive. I will be working. Anna is taking a leave of absence. She needs it. When I finish work, we'll be out and about out. And yes, we will have someone with us."

David nodded as he listened to the couple's plans, adding his comments as well. Jeremiah rose at last, having spent time praying with David.

That evening, Jeremiah reached for Anna's hand as he stood by his car. They were out on a date, heading for a popular Italian restaurant. They both paused as they heard a commotion behind them and turned. They watched as four of Abe's team surrounded two men who protested loudly at being stopped. They also watched as plain clothes officers moved in and made the arrest that was so badly needed. The couple exchanged a glance before Anna stared around. She nodded to herself as she saw Will and Bob standing near them but with their backs to them. They had volunteered to be there that night to watch out for the couple.

Late that night, Anna set aside her phone. Bessie had called just to confirm details for Saturday and then to pray for Anna. Anna was grateful for that. She was very much afraid of what the next few days would bring. Her fear was that one of the little ones would be hurt.

Jeremiah stood at his front window. He had no lights on in the house, knowing that he was soon to retire except for that car parked at the curb in front of his house. It was not one of his friends or someone who was watching out for him. It belonged to his enemy. The man himself was out there. Jeremiah decided that he must have few men left who would work for him. Instead of retiring, Jeremiah found his prayer corner and spent the night in petitioning for the safety of his beloved Anna and her family and waiting in the presence of his Father. He rose with dawn's light with the assurance that God had heard him.

The next three days passed relatively quietly. Both Anna and Jeremiah had spied the man watching them but also saw him being watched as well. They knew from David that he was frantically confirming what new information was being provided. Emma was forwarding a raft of material that was helping to form a picture of just how vile a man they were after.

Saturday found Ardan's home a beehive of activity. Ardan watched as Jeremiah paced, knowing it was nerves but also fear about Anna. He reached to hug Jeremiah, surprising that man before he prayed for him.

Anna too had her share of nerves, not about marrying Jeremiah but about what they were facing. It was not over. By marrying, they had likely just added fuel to the fire.

A week passed since Anna and Jeremiah married. They had sent home the security teams, simply stating that they could not be with them all that time. They had lives of their own to live. Jeremiah had made the decision to leave his home for now and live in the condo. They had better security when they were home there. No one got in or out unless they were residents there or had been allowed into the building. They had seen the man pacing outside the building, frustrated that he could not get to them.

That Sunday, Anna paused as they were heading for Jeremiah's car. Something was off and she just didn't know what. Her hand pulled Jeremiah to a stop.

———

He frowned at her before his mouth opened and then closed. He watched the men approaching them and frantically looked for a way out.

Anna sensed that something was off around them and tugged Jeremiah with her as she began to run away from the condo building and towards the downtown area. She knew that Will and Bob were on duty that day, Will sending her a text message to find them if they needed to hide. And to find them was what Anna was determined to do.

Jeremiah looked around in surprise as a group of street people suddenly surrounded them and moved them away from their pursuers and through a number of derelict buildings. Anna simply shrugged at him at the question on his face. This was not the first time that this had happened to people that she knew. Anna was well aware that if you treated these people as humans and with kindness, they would repay that.

Finally coming to a stop near Jeremiah's home, Anna and Jeremiah looked around. They were on their own. Sharing a look, Jeremiah moved to walk towards his house, stopping as Anna's hand landed on his arm.

"Wait, Jeremiah. He's out there, waiting for us. We can't go into the house." Anna shot a look around before she was running away from that area, Jeremiah following her.

"Where are we heading?" Jeremiah's hand finally landed on her arm and pulled her to a stop.

"We're heading for David's home. You know? The investigator? He lives near here. He should be home." Anna carefully studied the house in front of her and then the surrounding area before she was running for the back yard and then approaching the back door.

David stared at the two as they appeared on his back deck. He shook his head. Something had happened to drive them there and he wanted to know what.

____

Chapter 39

David paced his kitchen watching Anna and Jeremiah closely. It had not surprised him that an attempt had been made once more on the couple. He just feared for their lives if they were to disappear. Anna in turn watched David, waiting for just what she wasn't sure. Jeremiah had slumped into a chair, desperation in his demeanour. He had felt sure that when they married, they would be left alone. Obviously, that was not the case.

Anna walked away from the two men, intent on just what she wasn't sure. She had been a guest in David's house more than once, many times as a guest of his wife. Mary was away on a vacation with her parents and for some reason, Anna was glad for that. She had no idea what was coming but she could feel the storm clouds gathering.

Hearing a sound at the front door, Anna glanced towards where David stood in deep conversation with Jeremiah and then crept that way. She was not prepared for the heavy banging at the door or the sound of glass as it broke and tinkled on the floor. Anna's scream split the air before David was shoving her and Jeremiah through the kitchen and into the garage. He barely waited for them to be in his truck before he had the truck in reverse. He hardly cleared the raising garage door as he hit the accelerator and then spun the wheel to head forward. Anna watched in horror as the wizened old man standing on the front porch raised a weapon.

"He's got a gun! David!" Anna ducked as Jeremiah shoved her to the floor, his body covering hers.

"I know. Stay down!" David's foot pressed down on the pedal as he raced away from his home, heading for safety or so he prayed. His truck skidded sideways as he made the turn into the precinct parking lot. He hardly had the truck in park before officers surrounded it and raced the couple inside to safety.

Unlocking his office door, David shoved the two into it and motioned for an officer to stand in the doorway. His phone was out to send a message to his wife not to come home and why. He then strode towards the break room, tracking down the detective he needed and sending him to his home. David sighed. This was to have been a relaxing day off and that had not happened.

Anna turned to watch the hallway, not sure as to what had just happened. Jeremiah had her wrapped as tightly in his arms as he could. She could hear his prayer raising for them and then added her own.

"Was that really him?" Anna's quiet question broke through the silence in the office.

"It was, Anna." David had reappeared. "Sit. We need to talk." He watched as Anna glared at him for a moment before she sat, her chair as close to Jeremiah's as she could get it. "He has been following you closely. From what we have determined, he no longer has anyone willing to work for him. That has made him desperate. And today is a result of that desperation."

———

Jeremiah and Anna had to agree. That was the conclusion that they had reached early that morning. Neither had been able to sleep, instead rising and spending their time in prayer. They had walked away from the condo that morning with confidence that God was in control and that their adventure as it was termed would be over soon. Abe and Emma had reached out overnight with confirmation of who they faced and a guess on Abe's part as to why. The couple had looked at each other in shock. They had not dreamed that could be a reason why.

David studied his friend. He could see the subtle changes in her and disliked them. He looked up at the tap on his door and beckoned Joe in.

Anna was on her feet, giving Joe a hug before she walked away, Jeremiah following her. She was gone before David fully realized that she was leaving. He and Joe scrambled to find them without success.

"Where would they go?" David stood with a hand on his head. He was having trouble reading Anna at this point.

"To Jeremiah's house. They are ready to make a stand and have this over with. It has gone on for far too long and taken too much from them." Joe walked away, heading for his car and then to find the couple.

David watched Joe leave, frustrated that he had to stay and deal with the incident at his home. All he could do was pray for his friends, bathing them in a plea for God's protection.

Jeremiah hesitated for a moment as he stared at his house. He felt Anna's hand tighten on his as they waited. Just what they were watching and waiting for, he wasn't sure. Finally, he walked towards the back door and unlocked it, pulling Anna in with him and locking the door behind them. The air in the house was stale and stuffy, given that the house had been closed up for a week.

"Jeremiah?" Anna's voice held the question that she would not ask.

"I know, Anna. I know. He will be out there waiting for us. We make our stand here. Richard and Don and their teams are out there. They will let him through, moving in to cover us. Abe can't be here today but Emma has forwarded what she has and the proof to David." Jeremiah paced, knowing that they would face that man as Anna called him at some point during the day. They had chosen the date and place, knowing that he would appear. An ad in the local newspaper would ensure that. It had not been planned that he showed up at David's.

A sound at the front door had Anna covering her mouth with both hands to stifle her scream. Her eyes were huge as Jeremiah hugged her. A finger to his lips kept her quiet. He crept towards the hallway where he could see the door. His head dropped as he saw the man causing all their troubles standing there. His phone vibrated with a message from Richard that they were moving in. Would Jeremiah and Anna please stay put and not confront the man?

Anna and Jeremiah shared a look. To confront the man had been exactly what they wanted to do and had planned on. But with Richard requesting that they not, they were well aware that something was going

on. Jeremiah simply replied to Richard's message that
they would stay safe. But they wanted details on what
was going on.

Chapter 40

A week later, Joe and David walked towards Ardan's home. It was finally over, they commented to one another. There had been a tangled web many years in the making that had in turn taken days to unravel.

Ardan waited for them on the front porch. Not satisfied with just a handshake, he reached to hug the two detectives. He felt that they had indeed been used by God to bring resolution to an adventure that had taken too many years from his sister and her now groom.

"Thank you, David and Joe. You have brought closure for these two. Our prayers are with you as you work through the final stages. It certainly has not been what we imagined."

"No, it has not." David watched the group gathered in the house. "Everyone is here?"

"They are. They want to hear the reasons why and to know that the danger is over." Ardan followed them into the house. "First, we have a meal ready to share. Then we want to spend time in prayer."

Joe found the triplets, watching as they reacted with the men of the security teams. These teams had been involved in the adventures as they were called that they had undergone. He saw the two ladies from Richard's team with the younger wives.

Anna was on her feet, wrapping Joe into a hug. Tears sparkled briefly in her eyes as she could not find the words to thank him audibly.

Laughter and happiness flowed through the house once more. It had seemed to have taken too long for that to happen. Ardan watched his much loved and adored little sister, seeing the peace and happiness in her that had been missing. He had not realized the burden and pain that his sister had carried for all those years. She had hidden it well. To have Jeremiah back in her life had released her. That he loved her deeply was obvious to everyone.

Abe stood for a moment when the meal was finished, waiting for quiet to come over the room. He then simply bowed his head and began their time of prayer. Richard drew the time to a close, ending his prayer with his usual "I love You". Everyone afterwards said that they felt the presence of God in the room in a way that they had never in the past. When questioned on how he ended his prayers, Richard would just say that God loved them and that they needed to tell Him that they loved Him.

Anna shared a look with Jeremiah even as he wrapped her tighter in his arms. They had lost a lot of years to that man as she referred to him as. They just didn't have the whole picture and desperately wanted to know why he had done what he did.

Joe had taken a seat near her, his parents close to him. He watched her closely as well, seeing the relief she was now experiencing. His eyes then turned to Jeremiah and saw that he was beginning to heal from his ordeal. And that was what it had been, an ordeal that God had allowed. No one was sure as to the reason. Joe was well aware that they might never know on earth.

"David?" Anna's quiet voice broke through the silence that had remained in the room. "What can you tell us?" Her hands tightened on Jeremiah's. They had come so close to losing one another forever. God had protected them and brought Jeremiah home once more. They were both changed from what they had been as young adults. They could never go back to that but had to move forward as they now were.

"What can we tell you?" David shared a look with Joe. "I'll let Joe talk first. He's been the one who has been digging into past history, with thanks to Emma for her assistance in this."

Joe nodded. It had taken time to dig into what the reason had been and it went back to when Anna and Jeremiah were teenagers. He had not expected that at all.

"This goes back a long way, Anna, Jeremiah. Back to when you were teenagers. Are you familiar with Joyce Whyte?"

Anna turned her face to Jeremiah, a frown on her face. Jeremiah was shaking his head.

"I don't know her. Should we?" Anna was puzzled by the question.

"Not necessarily, but she knows you two. Her father is Larry Waite. She uses her mother's name. Her mother is Suzanne Whyte." Joe looked over at Ardan as he made a sound. "Ardan?"

"Her? She's been in and out of trouble for so many years. The last I heard was that Suzanne was in jail for drug possession." Ardan's hand gripped Bessie's.

"She has been. More times that she should have been but she has never learnt her lesson. Her daughter, Joyce, has resented the fact that Anna and Jeremiah had parents who loved them and provided a stable God-fearing home for them. She is under arrest in another town for assault and break and enter. She won't be out for quite a while." Joe reached for his bottle of water, sipping at it, and then recapping it. He rolled it in his hand for a moment, not sure how to continue.

"There's more, isn't there, Joe?" Anna's voice was low but held confidence that there was.

"There is, Anna. I am not quite sure how to continue." Joe shared a look with David who nodded. "The man who was behind it all? The man who tried to confront you last week? His name is not what we know him by. We know him as Joel Lloyd. That is an alias that he took years ago. Your parents would have known him as Terence Lewis."

There were shocked voices sounding through the room as they realized who it had been. Anna turned to Emma who nodded. She had finally been able to work through all the road blocks that Lewis had built around himself and his criminal empire.

"Yes, him. David, you took over the investigation after he tried to break into your home." Joe turned to his supervisor.

"That I did. We were able to weed through all his lies and attempts of cover up. Jeremiah, he was the one truly behind what you went through. John from the team that brought you home has provided the proof that we needed on the man who held you captive. It was his nephew who led his criminal team overseas. They planned to make you work for them. After a certain number of years, they would send you home but provide proof that you were involved in criminal activities. You never went along with them. That resulted in your long captivity. The other captives are free. The authorities over there are working through all the evidence. Your witness spread widely and it became common for anyone that was taken captive to refuse to work with them.

"As to why you went through it all? Jealousy and greed. You two were planning a life with one another. Joyce wanted what you had and didn't have it. The men in her life tried to make it happen. Only it didn't. They forgot that only God can provide the life that you two led. You remained true to one another over the years. You also remained true to God. He fought your fight and reunited you two in His timing. God has blessed your witness over the years."

Ardan shared a look with his sister before he hesitated to speak.

"Jeremiah? Did John or Chris or Greg ever say how they found you? Someone has to have known where you were." That was a question that puzzled all of them.

Jeremiah stared at Ardan for a moment before his arm tightened around Anna. They had discussed it as a couple and had come to no real conclusion.

"No, they never did. When I asked them, they just shrugged. They won't tell me if they do know. It's how they work. They simply stated that someone knew where I was and asked them to go in and bring me home. That it was time that I came home and reunited with Anna. That she had grieved long enough." Jeremiah had to work to control his emotions. "I not likely will ever know but God worked it all out for us. We didn't like what we had to go through, but He had ultimate control over our lives and what He allowed to happen."

Joe and David walked away from the house not too much longer after that. The three security teams did as well, hugging both Anna and Jeremiah. Jeremiah's boss had hugged Anna and then Jeremiah. He would speak with Jeremiah in the coming weeks, surprising that man with his words.

Anna and Jeremiah walked away from their family in the early evening. They needed to find some place quiet just to come to terms with what they had been told. Jeremiah had kissed his bride as he tucked her into his car, grateful that they were together and more in love than they had been as a young couple.

Two years later, Anna sat on the back deck of their home. She and Jeremiah had decided to live in the house that he had purchased and use her condo as short-term lodgings for those in need. Today, family and friends had gathered to celebrate. David had sold his jewelry business to Jeremiah, despite Jeremiah's protests that it should go to one of the others. None of them had wanted it, knowing that it had been David's wish for all those years that Jeremiah take it over. Jeremiah had a rare talent for designing jewelry that they seldom saw but he didn't hesitate to train and teach the others if they asked. And he was asked.

Anna's gaze tracked among the family. Everyone else had left, leaving just the ones closest to her in their back yard. She found Arlyn's little girl, Ayrin, playing with the tri-coloured Sheltie pup that Jeremiah had surprised her with a couple of weeks previously. Her giggles and laughter brought smiles to all of those near her.

Her gaze then found Briar's young son, Baird, hard at play in the sandbox that Jeremiah had created for their nieces and nephews. Cayce's young son, Cam, played just as hard as his cousin. These two were great pals, crying when they had to be separated to go home.

Next, she watched Cayce's young daughter, Cadi, as she sat on the lawn, peals of giggles coming from her. Anna's calico kitten tumbled and played around her. This little girl loved her animals and always searched for the kitten when she was at her aunt's.

Anna sat in silence for a moment as she watched the younger ladies gathered in a group. Joe's wife, Natalie, was there. Joe was considered family and was always welcome to any gatherings. His parents had been there but had had to leave for another commitment.

Anna's face was wreathed in happiness and peace. She looked down as she felt a tug at her skirt and her hand rested on the brown curls of the little girl who danced up and down. She reached to wipe away the drool from her daughter's face. They had not expected to become parents but little Deree was the pride and joy of her parents.

Her gaze then found Bessie and Ardan as they stood near her rose garden, watching their grandchildren playing. They were happy that now life had resumed a normalcy that had been missing for years. Anna watched at Bessie cuddled Anna and Jeremiah's young son, Evan, as he slept. Evan played hard and slept hard. He was a blessing as well to his parents.

Lastly, she found Jeremiah, who stood near her, their youngest cuddled in his arms as she watched the activity around her. Little Fae might be the youngest of the triplets but she made up for that. For yes, Jeremiah and Anna had been blessed with triplets. They had not expected three but they cherished each one. Ardan had laughed long and hard at his sister when she told him, simply stating that she couldn't let him get ahead of her for children. This set of triplets knew that they were loved and loved in return.

That evening, Anna quietly stepped from the nursery, leaving the door open. Jeremiah wrapped her into his arms, kissing her and then turning them to walk down the stairs. He had set up a snack for them in the sunroom. Anna was grateful for the husband that she had who provided for their family and as a father, led their children in a loving manner.

"Okay, sweetheart?" Jeremiah wrapped her into his arms again as they sat.

"I am, love. I am. I think that finally after all these years, I am. God has provided for us in so many ways. He protected you during your captivity and led others to Himself because of your witness. Who knows who you were to reach because of what you endured."

Jeremiah nodded. Anna was correct. They had no idea of how far his witness may have reached.

"What next? You have quit your job." He watched her beloved face closely as he spoke.

Anna nodded. She had no desire to go back to work and had not worked since they married. Her family was her priority. She also mentored teenage girls and found that provided the part of her life that was needed.

"I am happy just being at home. The triplets are at that stage when they are so delightful to be around even when they are mischievous." She looked up at

Jeremiah. "I love you, Jeremiah. I never stopped even when I grieved not having you with me."

Jeremiah kissed her and then laid his head on hers.

"I love you too. I thought that when I returned you would have moved on and married. God meant for us to be together."

There was silence in the room, a peaceful quiet. They knew that God had protected them and provided for them. It was Who He was and what He did. They could only trust Him to continue to lead in their lives.

Thank you for choosing to read *Reunited. Anna's Story*. It was an unplanned novel, a hint dropped of a story that Aunt Anna had to tell in *Keeping Humble*, Cayce's story. Once more, the characters didn't let the author in on the full story, choosing instead to let it come out as the fingers were on the keyboard.

This story was to have been my April Camp Nanowrimo novel but life got in the way. An unexpected fall and shoulder fracture meant that didn't happen and almost 20,000 words have been written with just the left hand. God was there in this story, leading in how it developed, as always.

For the characters who love to walk into others' adventures? Abe's team in *His Guardians*. Richard's team is *His Protectors*. Don's team is *His Defenders*. Blackie and Simon are part of *Mistletoe Treasures*. I try not to let them come into other's stories but they just walk in and take over, moving the plot line along.

For the triplets, their stories are the trilogy, *In God's Keeping*. Arlyn's is *Keeping Justice*, Briar's *Keeping Mercy*, and Cayce's *Keeping Humble*.

Events happen to us during our life. We don't know the reason why sometimes. God does. He uses us to reach others with a message that He has for them. We may never know the impact of our walk with Him on earth. He does protect and provide for us in ways that we don't expect or even realize that we need. God can and will reunite people. He has plans and purposes that we don't know about as a favourite character is wont to say. All we can do is trust Him and follow as He leads.

And a thank you to my sister for taking time to proofread for me.

God bless each one of you as you travel this path called Life. Keep your hand in His.

Ronna

www.ingramcontent.com/pod-product-compliance
Lightning Source LLC
Chambersburg PA
CBHW060446310726
48977CB00001B/338